Spiraling

RACHEL CROSS

Author of *Rock Her* and *Rock Him*

CRIMSON
ROMANCE

F+W Media, Inc.

This edition published by
Crimson Romance
an imprint of F+W Media, Inc.
10151 Carver Road, Suite 200
Blue Ash, Ohio 45242
www.crimsonromance.com

ISBN 10: 1-4405-7487-1
ISBN 13: 978-1-4405-7487-0
eISBN 10: 1-4405-7488-X
eISBN 13: 978-1-4405-7488-7

For Anna, Anne, Kirsten, Kristen, Steff,
and John, and my editor, Julie Sturgeon.

Acknowledgments

Acknowledgments: Chris, my inspiration. Monica Tillery, Kai, Jenny, Kathy and Mark, thanks for keeping it real. Judy M. and Cheree, thank you for taking care of vital parts of my life while I wrote. Finally, heartfelt thanks to my Crimson Romance team, especially Tara Gelsomino.

Chapter One

An odd snapping sensation and a rush of slick heat accompanied his final thrust. A thrust that seated him balls deep in disaster. Shane Marx retracted his hips, removed his hands from the smooth, firm ass and took two stumbling steps away from the woman on her hands and knees on the edge of the bed. Too late. He stared down in horror at the remnants of the condom, still attached at the base, a wide tear splitting the tip.

Motherfucker.

The woman's body trembled from the effects of his exertions.

His heart rate ratcheted up. "Uh." He racked his brain for a name. Nope. Nothing. Given how swiftly things proceeded at the club, he wasn't sure they'd exchanged that information. She knew who he was, and after thirty minutes of foreplay in the guise of dancing, she'd been eager to get him back to her place.

"We may have a problem," he said.

The woman belly flopped onto floral sheets, then rolled over with a satisfied groan. She looked at him, her face slack with the remnants of pleasure and fatigue, mascara smeared almost to her cheeks. She pushed tangled blonde hair off her damp face. "What?"

Following his gaze she spotted the ruined condom and her eyes widened. Her hand investigated the apex of her thighs and she giggled.

He clenched his teeth.

"Oh." Her smile was coy. "You don't have to worry. I'm clean."

"Yeah? That's good. Me too." But that wasn't his greatest concern, and from the calculating gleam in her eye, she knew it.

He pressed his palm to his forehead as fears of paternity suits, child-custody hearings, and tabloid photos throbbed to life.

What were the odds? Slim to maybe? He had never, ever had a condom failure. TruAchord would have been dead on arrival if he or any of his boy-band mates had been hit with a paternity suit back in the day. Years later he was still neurotic about using them.

Shane backed up until he was in the attached bathroom. He peeled off and flushed the condom. "Are you on the pill or anything?" he called out. When he came back into the room she was kneeling on the bed, holding up her iPhone to take a picture of him. He covered himself with both hands, took two strides forward, and wrested the phone from her grasp. He flipped through her photos, deleting the fuzzy one she'd taken as his heart thundered in his chest.

"Hey!"

He glared at her. "So not cool."

His agent would have a seizure if more naked photos emerged. The one some twit sent out last month had been bad enough. "Good God, Shane! Who wants to see a full frontal of you *sleeping*? At least the quarterbacks and politicians have the decency to get photos of their *erections*. Don't get me wrong, we should count ourselves lucky you're a show-er and not a grower, but this is a disaster! I'm having a hell of a time passing this off as a Photoshop job."

Apparently there was such a thing as bad publicity, and that picture had killed his audition for a lead in the latest Sparks film. No matter. He was done being typecast as the guy with issues in all that chick-flick crap. Maybe that photo would put him in consideration for a grittier role, but two? Two photos would indicate he had a problem. He held her phone while he slipped on his jeans. He pocketed it, and then checked his pants for wallet, keys, and his phone. Two steps across matted beige carpeting took him to the doorway where he spared her a glance.

She frowned at him from where she stood, naked beside the bed, one hand on a curvaceous hip, the other stroking through highlighted extensions. She spent way too much time in the tanning booth. The florescent light from the bathroom gave her skin a terracotta glow.

Revulsion surged through him.

"Are you on the pill or not?" he repeated.

"No."

"Is there something you can take? You know, so there aren't any unwanted repercussions?"

She shrugged. "Probably."

"Do you want me to set something up?" Should he offer her money or would that piss her off?

"I'll take care of it," she assured him, breaking eye contact.

His gut clenched. There wasn't much he could do at four in the morning. Or anytime for that matter. It wasn't as though he could march her to the pharmacy or a doctor's office or wherever.

Shane glanced around the room for clues to the woman's psyche. Neat, and decorated with some flair—though the bureau and nightstand screamed thrift store special. Poor, not slovenly.

It was always the same. The initial thrill, diminishing interest as things progressed to the point of no return, and the emptiness and awkwardness after. Now fear had entered the equation.

"Will you give me back my goddamn phone?" she said, extending a hand.

Shane turned his back on her and hustled through the apartment. He pulled a wad of bills from his money clip and chucked them along with her phone in the vicinity of the stained sofa. He made his way down the stairs of the second story garden apartment and onto the street. He'd been so distracted by her head bobbing in his lap in the back seat of the taxi he hadn't the faintest idea where he was. His phone showed him standing smack in the middle of Brantley, eight miles and several worlds away from his Santa Monica neighborhood. He turned west and started his jog of shame home.

Chapter Two

Two weeks later Shane sat in his living room across from rock megastar Asher Lowe—one of his more incongruous friendships.

"Fuck, man." Asher shook his head. "There's gotta be something you can do. Go to her apartment and talk to her. Give her money. Something."

"I left her some money. A couple hundred. I'm playing the odds." He ran a hand across his face.

Asher stared at him in disbelief. "Dude, that's a bad bet."

"Seriously, what are the chances? One night, one busted condom. I've looked it up. It's unlikely."

Asher studied him. "Take my word on this. It's a tough thing to share a child with a stranger, and we both know more than most people about lousy parents. Step up and talk her into taking measures."

"Asher, I don't know her name."

"Yeah. About that ... "

Shane stared at his friend and gave a short laugh. "This outta be good. A lecture on fidelity from the biggest man-whore on the planet?"

"Former man-whore," Asher retorted. "Since reformed. You might consider it, you know. Sleeping with someone regularly. Having a real relationship, with someone not in the industry."

"God. There's no one more pious than a reformed sinner."

"I had more than my share of good times, back in the day, but this thing with Maddy, well, it's on another level," Asher said.

"I suck at monogamy. Seriously suck at it. I can't imagine choosing to be with one person long term and continually saying no to the newest thrill."

"Thrill?"

"Yeah." Shane shifted in his chair. "You know how it is when you first meet someone you want to fuck? The excitement? It feels like gearing up to hit the stage, until after ... "

Shane felt Asher's eyes on him as he examined his uneaten roast beef sandwich. Asher must understand this cycle he was in—had been in as long as he could remember. But then, unlike Shane, Asher's past was littered with bouts of monogamy and fidelity, even before he fell for Maddy.

When he looked up, Asher was still observing him, his brilliant hazel eyes lit with keen intelligence and compassion.

"It wasn't a thrill ... not like you describe. Sex was never an urge I had regrets about. Sure, there were some needy women, but I learned how to deal with them without alienating them—diplomacy and tact go a long way, although there are always the clingers—and I learned to spot the unbalanced from fifty feet. Most of them knew the drill. Some women I enjoyed for more than sex—women I had relationships with. But not the whacked-across-the-head-with-a-two-by-four experience. Not until Maddy. Speaking of, I've got to get back to Vegas." He looked at his phone. "Jet's fueled up. Can you run me over to the airport?" Asher stood. "Go see the girl. Find out where she's at."

Shane also stood and dangled his keys. Screw that. He was sick of both being used and using women to work out something—fill some hole. The very last thing he was going to do was beg Ms. Nameless to do the right thing. Besides, there was no way she could be pregnant after that one time.

Fucking condom.

A few hours after he dropped Asher at the airport and had returned to his couch, his phone rang. He used the remote to pause Tristan Brennan's latest film and stared at the number on the screen.

Ike Peters, super-agent. His stomach lurched.

"Hey, man," Shane answered with studied casualness. As if he hadn't been waiting for this call for weeks.

"Shane, you're a real pain in my ass."

Shane closed his eyes and did a fist pump. "What else is new?" *Get to the point.*

But it paid to play the game. Even with his own agent he locked down his excitement.

"I've got a line in to get you that audition."

Shane's heart leapt into his throat with a combination of joy and panic.

"God! Thank you," he breathed reverently, not sure if he was actually thanking God or his agent who thought he was God.

"They're having issues getting funding of course, and it doesn't pay shit. You'll be working for scale," he moaned. "I'd have been much happier if you'd done the Sparks film, but you blew that. The Brennan picture will shoot some locally, some in Canada. Auditions are still a few months away—maybe the end of the year but spring more likely. I had to beg to get this done for you—let me tell you, after the shenanigans on your last picture, they're leery. *Everyone* is leery. You caused crisis after crisis because you couldn't keep your dick in your pants. I don't have any other clients like you. Fucking the co-star? *And* the special effects assistant? And a *local?* Do you have a death wish? If you ever do get a role again, they'll put it in your contract that you can't fuck co-stars or crew. They ain't groupies for your boy band, you know. This is a business, son."

Shane held his breath, fists clenched. It wasn't his fault the special effects chick had gone psycho. How was he to know she'd turn a one-night stand into a fantasy relationship and then try to sabotage the film during production?

"Are you there?"

"Yes," he replied softly.

"Well," the man huffed out. "You didn't tell me the character was a hockey player. Jesus, Shane, have you read the fuckin' script? Do you *know* how to ice skate?"

"Uh," he mumbled. How hard could it be? He was in great shape. A few lessons—he'd never had a problem picking up dance moves with TruAchord.

"Well you do now. That skating clause was a deal breaker, so I told them you were freakin' Brian Boitano. . ."

"Isn't he a figure skater?"

"Who cares? The important thing is you need to know how to fuckin' skate. And you don't. So you better fuckin' learn."

Shane was already reaching for his laptop, ready to search for ice skating coaches.

"And on the down low, so don't even think about going through regular channels for that. Leave it to me. We can't have word getting out that you're taking lessons, for Chrissake."

"Just to brush up," he said feebly, shutting his laptop.

"Fuckin' Boitano doesn't need to brush up! I'll take care of it. Clear your schedule," he ordered. "Now here's what you are gonna do for me ... "

•••

Amelia Astor closed her eyes and tilted her face to the sun.

"Hey, Amy."

She grinned.

Kyle Reed had the world's sexiest voice—a husky baritone that was a perfect match for his chiseled features and sculpted body. After years of clinches, embraces, throws, and spins, she was as familiar with his body as her own.

People turned to stare at him. Fewer noticed here in LA than in other places in the world they had traveled together where their matched blonde heads stood out, but they were used to stares.

Did they suspect brother and sister? They shared light blue eyes, too—though his were shot with glass-green. They shared the same Slavic cheekbones. Maybe they shared a common ancestry, other than the obvious.

She put her latte on the glass-top, wrought iron table, and stood to give him a full-body hug, her hands gripping his back muscles, reveling in his familiar smell. He gave her a chaste kiss on the lips.

"Missed you," she said. The little house they shared with another Enchanted skater, Allyson, had seemed terribly empty during his absence. Cleaner of course—Kyle wasn't known for his housekeeping skills—but far too quiet.

"Me too, babe."

"Mmmm. What is that? Cinnamon something?" He seated himself across from her.

"Yeah." She pushed her cup toward him.

"Nah. I'll get a coffee in a minute. Any word?"

"Not yet," she said, worrying her lower lip with her teeth. "I'm sure I'll hear from them soon. Enchanted is scheduled to go back on tour ... mid-September, right?"

His expression was sober, his gaze probing. "Rehearsals start here in August."

Nine weeks away. All of the principals had received offer letters last week, everyone but her. Tears filled her eyes and she blinked them away. After seven years of playing the lead princess in the Enchanted Ice show, they were going to give her the boot. She wasn't ready, damn it. She would decide when her skating career was over, not the Enchanted management. Control was the one thing she had in the life she'd made for herself after a youth dictated by parents and coaches. She would put off real life one more year. She just had to find a way back in.

"How was home?"

He shrugged and looked away.

Amy leaned forward and gripped his fisted hand.

He managed a half smile and threaded his fingers through hers. "Fuck 'em," she advised.

He shook his head, expression glum. "Why can't I follow your lead and cut them off?"

She squeezed his wide palm and let go. "Maybe because you have siblings. It must be a stronger bond than I had with only my parents in the picture. I've said it before—"

"I know, Amy, 'people who make us feel bad about things that bring us joy don't love us in a healthy way,'" he mimicked her high voice.

She laughed. "Right. Is it the college thing or the 'he must be gay thing'?"

"The college thing. They've given me all kinds of permission to come out to them."

She giggled. "I'm sorry, but it's so funny."

"I know, right? I mean, they're my parents, they're supposed to know me. I couldn't give a good goddamn if anyone thinks I'm gay, but it comes up every time I'm home. I tell them … I'm not gay! I get why, there are plenty of gay dudes figure skating. Some of the best. So what if I play a prince? I love it. But gay guys never hit on me—*they* know I'm straight, while my own parents are freakin' clueless. I've fucked half the women in LA, but I must be closeted."

"About that—"

"Don't start," he warned. "I'm not in the mood to be slut-shamed."

She met his gaze until he couldn't hold hers any longer.

"Kyle, I know it used to be fun—"

"It still is," he insisted. "Amy, spare me the lectures. I've had ten days of my mom wringing her hands over her son's miserable excuse for a life. My siblings all have master's degrees or law degrees. And apparently, I'm not just the black sheep, I'm the closeted black sheep."

"I'm sorry. You know I love you, but I don't think an infinite parade of women—"

He held up a hand, the look in his eyes warning her not to go there. "Love you too, Amy. Let me get a coffee. You want anything?"

She should, she'd barely managed more than a salad yesterday. The stress of waiting for that letter—for her future—had tied her stomach in knots. And she would not gain an ounce; in fact, if she lost, it might help take some of the strain off her injured hip. Amy shook her head and watched Kyle go—her gaze not the only one following his retreating figure, judging by the craned necks on the patio.

She was used to envious glances. She was used to more than envy. She'd been the object of a jealous rage or two when whoever Kyle was seeing got the wrong idea about the two of them. Not only did they look like siblings, Kyle was the closest thing to family she had. And now that family—the set designers, the crew, the other skaters including Kyle—would go on the road without her as the Enchanted Ice powers-that-be kicked her to the curb.

The principal in an ice show had to either be a draw or young, healthy, and inexpensive. Amelia Astor had been a draw for Enchanted for eight years ever since she'd left the competitive circuit virtually on the eve of the Olympics, the top-ranked American woman skater. She'd run away to join the ice show, but at twenty-six she was getting a little long in the tooth to play a princess.

Then there were the injuries. The stress fractures, sprains, and strains from missed jumps in her youth as a U.S. junior ladies champion on the National Figure Skating circuit, were a legacy of aches and pain she would always carry. They were manageable, but there was a little something missing from her performances these days. And she couldn't continue the cortisone injections when her hip got bad forever.

It was time to move on with her life as Amy Astor. Settle down, go to college. Figure out a career. There was no home on the road, and these summers living in a group house in Los Angeles with skaters and crew wasn't it either. It was time to say good-bye to Amelia Astor, Enchanted princess. But not quite yet.

Kyle returned with his coffee and a bagel egg sandwich, sitting down across from her.

"Want me to talk to them?" he asked around a mouthful of food.

Her stomach rumbled and she took another sip of her coffee. "No. I don't want to seem desperate. There's still a chance."

He cocked his head. "Why *are* you desperate, doll? You can do whatever. Coach?"

She gave him a narrow-eyed glare. "No, thanks."

"Commentate?"

"Kyle, it's not like I won a medal or anything."

"That's bullshit and you know it. You won plenty, just not *the* medal. People loved you. After all that negative press about women's figure skating—"

"You mean *ladies'* figure skating," she said with a tiny smile.

Kyle laughed. "Yeah, ladies figure skating got a bad rep for a while, and you were what the sport needed: drama-free athleticism combined with grace, power, and beauty. Flawless performances—"

"Oh, there was drama. The coaching changes when I hit puberty? And of course, at the end when I could barely finish my program because I was starving myself."

His lips twisted and he examined her critically. "You doing alright with that?"

"I'm okay."

"You look a little lean. Here." He pushed the other half of his bagel sandwich toward her.

Her stomach rumbled and she eyed it hungrily before pushing it back.

Inside, she was a teeming mass of nerves. If Enchanted didn't pick her up, what then? The only thing that relieved her anxiety about her future were long runs, and they were getting longer and longer, while her hip got achier and achier. Then again she'd rarely been in better shape, so when they did pick her up. . .

"So, commentating?" Kyle was asking.

"It's been ages. I'm telling you, people don't remember me."

"So? Remind them. You're the gorgeous, great blue-blooded hope who went out at the top of your game. People know you could've bagged an Olympic medal for us. You come up every four years, and this is an Olympic year. I'm sure one of the networks would—"

"Kyle. No coaching. No commentating. It's not me. Can you see me blathering endlessly about program music, costumes, and skater backstory?"

"No. But I can't see you playing a princess for the rest of your life either, even if they do sign you for another year."

Amy tossed her hair back. "There are other shows."

His mouth dropped open. Kyle set his coffee on the table carefully and covered her hand. "No. No way, Amy. Most of those shows are—we both know how bad things can be with some of the other shows." He squeezed her hand. "Enchanted may be the circus, but it has a good reputation. It's safe, and management takes decent care of us here and overseas. We've both heard the stories about how sketchy the other shows are: low pay, nasty trailers, drunk performers, dangerous stunts. No. You need to figure out your retirement plan. I know you've thought about it. Why else would you have taken community college courses every summer? How many credits do you have now?"

"Twenty-one."

"Good God. Maybe you should enroll for a full semester."

"Toward a degree in what?" She groaned and put her head in her hands. "Kyle, I have no idea where to go from here. I need one more year to figure things out."

"You said that last year."

"I know," she said through her fingers.

"Look, I'll tell them we're a package deal."

A disbelieving laugh escaped her. "Babe, no you won't. They're itching for a reason to let you go, too—you're almost as old as me and equally expensive."

Her cell rang and she took it from her bag. She didn't recognize the number so she held up a finger to Kyle as he nodded.

"Hello?"

"I'm trying to reach Amelia Astor."

Amy rolled her eyes at Kyle, who frowned.

"This is she. I go by Amy."

"Fine, fine," the impatient male voice on the other end said. "Listen, I need you to do something for me."

"Who is this?"

"Ike Peters."

"Okaaay." She widened her eyes and shrugged at Kyle.

"You don't know my name?" he said.

"No, sorry."

"Eh. You're not in the industry, are you? I'm an agent and I have a client who needs ice skating lessons."

"I can recommend some people who do that."

"I want you."

"I don't give lessons."

"No, you're a princess, right? In the ice show? That Enchanted thing?"

"Yes, well, not right now." *And maybe never again.*

"No?" the man's tone sharpened, "why not?"

17

"We don't do the shows in the summer. We're off every year from May till September."

"Terrific." He sounded relieved.

"But I still can't help you."

"Name your price."

"Uh, I don't have a price, because you see, I don't teach ice skating."

Kyle was staring at her, an amused expression on his face.

"Well you do now. Name your price, rink, and time."

"Who's your client?"

It was his turn to laugh, but it was humorless. "Oh no. We're not going there. Not until you've signed a confidentiality agreement."

"So if I help this woman—"

"Person."

" … person learn to skate, I book the rink time and set my price?"

Kyle was nodding, grinning, and mouthing "Yes."

"Whatever you want. As long as you make him proficient—no, more than that. I need him skilled. I'll hold back some of the payment—think of it as a bonus—if you do your job."

So this was an agent representing an actor?

"Okay."

"You don't talk to anyone. You don't mention my name. Or his. Ever. Got it?"

Amy made a face at Kyle. She could use the money. It sure beat waitressing to make ends meet, or looking for a full-time job in case Enchanted didn't pick her up. She'd have to figure out how much skating coaches charged and then triple it. This was Los Angeles.

"Gotcha. I'm sure I can figure out how to teach him the basics," she said.

"Not just the basics, he needs to be good. Really good."

She frowned. "Like ice dancing, throwing-partners-around good? 'Cause that's not gonna happen in a few weeks or months, no matter how much time he puts in."

"No, no. Not like that. Good. Forward, backward, fast. None of that figure skating crap."

He sounded offended and she bit her lip to hold in laughter. "So he's not playing a figure skater?"

"Hell no!"

"Ah. A hockey player."

There was a suspicious silence on the other end of the phone. When he replied his tone was irritated. "Can you do it?"

"I guess."

"Do you have a fax?"

"Nope."

"Give me your address. I'll courier over the information. But God help you if you breathe a word of this, I'll make sure they put your princess days on ice."

Threats? She swallowed another giggle. This town took itself so damn seriously. "I won't mention it to anyone," she agreed, attempting to hide the humor in her tone. She told him her address, and he hung up before she'd given him the zip code.

Amy studied her phone, then laid it on the table. "That was bizarre."

"So now you're a coach?"

"I'm giving some lessons."

"Who?"

"He wouldn't say—some actor. I'm sworn to secrecy. Of course, as soon as I know, I'll tell you since you'll take all my secrets to the grave."

"Did I hear you say rink time?"

"Oh yeah."

They exchanged high fives.

"I'll call around. The first few sessions he won't last more than an hour. And Frank's has a three-hour rental minimum. We can play for two hours after he leaves," she said.

Kyle had a contemplative expression on his face.

"What?"

"Enchanted would scoop you up if you're linked to a Hollywood actor."

Amy brightened. "They would, wouldn't they?"

"If they don't want you to reveal he's getting lessons, fine. But if you can get him out for a drink after practice and I took a few photos," he tapped his chin with a finger, "I could feed it to one of those websites ... hell, I can probably set up a Twitter account and send it out."

"I don't know, Kyle," she said, pulling and twisting a lock of hair. "He said to keep quiet or he'd ice my career."

Kyle laughed. "Too late."

"*Kyle.*"

"Well it is, or did he mean to do it with a Louisville slugger? That's so passé."

"God, no. You know how this town is. It's all about connections, not abject brutality. This isn't ladies' figure skating."

Chapter Three

Amy reached the rink at seven-thirty Sunday night, her legs still tired from her run and the grueling stair workout she'd put herself through. She'd had to work around a variety of bookings, but she'd managed to get rink time five days a week in the evenings, after the horrible LA traffic died down and before midnight. She'd settled on the Glendale rink. It was close to home, she knew and liked the staff, and Frank, the owner, would keep quiet.

She sat in her car waiting. Who would it be? Channing Tatum? Bradley Cooper? From all the cloak and dagger, the guy had to be A-list. She snapped the radio off and nervously drummed her fingers on the steering wheel. It wasn't that she'd never taught anyone to skate before, but she had never hobnobbed with actors whose agents set things up.

A low-slung silver sports car pulled into the lot, parked, and a tall, lean man wearing a Tennessee Titans baseball cap emerged. Amy pulled the key out of the ignition of her old beat-up Miata, nerves fluttering. She didn't recognize him from this distance. Grabbing the bag with her skates and extra clothes, she shoved her purse into it and slung it over her shoulder, locking the door to the car.

He watched her approach, shifting his own bag higher on his broad shoulders.

Wait. She did recognize him—that actor who looked like he spent the morning out on the waves, and the afternoons surrounded by bikini-clad babes. Piercing deep-set, light blue eyes in an oddly angular face; a scruffy, dark blonde almost-goatee— he wasn't classically handsome, and he looked better on the big screen. Up close he looked intense and humorless.

What the hell was his name? He'd been in one of those dark, angsty pictures—sci-fi or superhero? It had been out a year or two ago, and hadn't gotten the warmest reception. Her eyes narrowed. Wait a minute. *Was this the guy—?*

"Shane Marx," he said dryly.

Heat rose in her cheeks as she realized from his expression that he'd noticed she couldn't place him. And probably noticed when she did place him and why, judging from the long-suffering expression on his face now.

He was all over the Internet last month. That full frontal image of his perfectly sculpted nude, sleeping body had been everywhere. Someone had posted a link to the unedited version and she had clicked it, of course. Now that she'd seen him up close, it seemed likely the photo was the real deal, and that the chest under that teal Henley was physical perfection—the broad-shouldered and muscular physique of an Olympic swimmer. Oh my God. *This* was the guy she was going to teach to skate?

She gulped and strove for professionalism.

"Amy Astor," she said, sticking out a hand.

"Amy, not Amelia?"

"That's right."

His large, warm hand enveloped hers as they shook. He held it a smidgen too long, his assessment, blatant, expression, bland, and eyes, appreciative.

She withdrew her hand.

"Nice to meet you." Now that he'd said his name, she knew exactly who he was. Boy band singer turned actor. Not A-list but leading man material—he could definitely get her on with Enchanted if word got out. Maybe he would suggest a drink. But even while fantasies of Enchanted's call ran through her head as she turned toward the rink, the hair on the back of her neck stood up. She could feel his eyes on her and she whipped her head around.

His lascivious expression was gone in the blink of an eye as his face relaxed into less predatory lines.

He walked around her and held the door open.

"Thanks," she muttered. "You got hockey skates?"

He tapped his bag in answer.

"I'm going to talk to Frank, the owner, okay? You can get your skates on," she said, moving through the entryway.

He followed. "I think I need to talk to him, too."

She stopped, turned with her hand on her hip, blocking his way, her smile saccharine sweet. "It's okay. I've paid Frank enough to rent the rink *and* keep his mouth shut." She manufactured a giggle and added conspiratorially, "I've known him for *years*. He'll keep quiet if there's money to be made. I warned him that if word gets out, we'd have to go elsewhere." Amy pointed to the benches in a corner. "Put your skates on and I'll be right over." Her smile firmly in place, she waited as he rubbed a hand over his scruffy chin, considering her. Whatever he saw in her face must have convinced him, because he turned away.

Moments later, she returned and took a seat next to him on the bench. She laced her worn skates.

"Make sure you lace them tight, okay?" she said, eyeing his handiwork.

He grunted in response.

When he stood, she offered her arm with another smile.

He raised his brows. "I think I can make it there without falling on my ass," he said.

"Hold up," she said as Shane made a move to step onto the ice. "I want to go over a few things before we get out there. Did your agent tell you I haven't instructed much?"

"No," he said, his face settling into those expressionless lines.

This guy was a tough read. But she couldn't fail to notice he spent an inordinate amount of time scoping out her body when he probably thought she wasn't looking. Dealing with overly amorous males around the world had given her a sixth sense about men on the make. She'd need to straddle the line between professionalism and feigned interest.

"I can teach you the basics. But if my instruction is too fast or too slow, let me know. The last thing I want is for you to get hurt. The ice is unforgiving." Her hand went instinctively to her right hip and she gave it a rub. "Have you been on skates before?"

"Nope."

"Okay. Then we'll start at the very beginning and go slowly. We have time, right?"

"Enough."

Amy took a deep breath and stepped onto the ice. "When you step onto the ice, step sideways and hold the barrier. Put your feet into the shape of a V." She demonstrated. "We're going to work on penguin steps." She bent over to give her laces a final tug. When she raised her head he averted his eyes so quickly she realized he was checking her out again. In other circumstances she might find his blatant attention irritating. But if she could parlay his interest into a bite or a drink out after practice, she would be golden—just as Kyle suggested.

"You'll feel silly the first few lessons, but I'm sure you'll pick it up quickly," she said, trying to establish her professional boundaries.

Shane's head tilted and a suggestion of a grin pulled up the corner of his mouth.

God, he was attractive when he smiled. Unbidden, that photo popped into her head and her eyes drifted down to the front of his pants.

She froze, blinked, and dragged her gaze back up to his face, but he was more concerned with finding his balance on the skates than watching her wandering eyes.

Amy released the barrier and took a few more forward steps, arms extended in front of her, picking up her feet as she demonstrated the beginner's awkward shuffle. "Like this." She skated to the entryway. "Ready?"

Shane made his way onto the ice as she suggested. She skated backward as he penguin-stepped around the rink. He had remarkable grace for such a tall guy, and he was muscular in that lean, cut way that indicated an active lifestyle or lots of time at the gym with a personal trainer. He'd been a dancer with TruAchord and obviously kept himself in shape, so this shouldn't be too difficult.

"You're doing great," she chirped.

He shot her a dour look and raised his brows. "You don't need to watch every step I take. Why don't you go show me some of your famous moves?" He dismissed her with a hand and stumbled, recovering quickly, but not before she'd taken two gliding strides toward him.

His lips twisted. "You're not going to catch me if I fall—and falling is part of the deal, right?"

"Yep." Amy backed up, but not before she'd gotten a whiff of him. He smelled of oranges and cinnamon—a cologne maybe? She studied his strong jaw and the column of his neck.

I wonder if he smells even better up close.

Confident with his ability to make it around the perimeter, she took a warm-up lap. It was chilly teaching in the rink. Her leggings and top under the thin fleece jacket were not protecting her from the cold. She shivered and increased her speed, her body heating up after a few times around the rink.

He started his third lap under her watchful eye. His ankles were wobbling a bit and he was trying to add the glide to the step—too soon.

He picked up his pace and she accelerated over to him, but she didn't make it before he wiped out and landed on his ass with a "Fuck!"

Thankfully, he had been going fast enough to slide and didn't do any damage.

She offered her hand, but he ignored it, getting awkwardly to his feet.

Amy put herself directly in front of him. The spicy citrus smell was even more pronounced. Her nose twitched and she stared at the thick, strong column of his neck. Her body throbbed to life.

It was that goddamn penis picture. Her subconscious was salivating. It didn't help that she hadn't had even a hookup since long before Enchanted came off the road in May. A three-month dry spell was too long, apparently.

Amy tamped down her attraction. "Let's walk before we try to run, shall we?" She strove for encouraging, but her voice sounded overly perky even to her.

He's not a child.

"If you've never been on skates, it's going to take a bit of time to get to the glide stage," she tried again.

Shane cleared his throat. "I'm ready," he insisted.

"Okay, Shane. If you're that eager to move forward, let's try it this way." She glided away to demonstrate, her best encouraging smile firmly in place. "Keep your feet parallel. Use your right foot like this."

Shane did a credible glide across the ice.

"Good, good. Keep going. Remember to keep your weight distributed and your arms level with your hips, like mine. Yours are too high."

He mimicked her. "Like this?"

"Yeah, that's terrific. Now be sure to push off with the inside edge of the blade."

"Will my ankles ever feel stable?" he asked.

"Eventually, it takes a while though."

He grunted, making his way with more determination than grace across the ice.

"Stroke and glide. You should be good at that."

Now where did that come from?

She masked her discomfort with a vacant expression.

He glanced up, grinning. An honest to God, genuine smile that made her stomach flip. He was transformed when he smiled. His beautifully sculpted mobile mouth opened to reveal perfect white teeth, crystalline blue eyes framed by eyelashes so dark they seemed incongruous with his dark blond hair—hair threaded with very expensive highlights or an excess of time in the California sun. Now she could see how he was leading man material—it hadn't been evident in his tight-lipped countenance before.

"Oh yeah? Could be I know something about that." He gave her another of those predatory glances.

She widened her eyes, striving for guilelessness. "Well, you *are* a dancer, right?"

He turned away, but not before she saw him shake his head.

This could be fun. She rarely got to play the ditz anymore since she was the tour veteran—*mamacita* Kyle called her. The veterans had looked out for her when she was the rookie, now she returned the favor.

"Once we have a reasonable glide, we'll work on the crossover for the coming weeks. It's a little trickier. You might want to get some pads."

Shane glanced up from his perusal of her body and lifted his brows. "I don't need pads."

Amy pressed her lips together, holding back her retort.

Narrowing her eyes, she skated up in front of him until he had to stop. She surveyed him critically, reaching out a hand to run it down the front of his chest. She gave him another thousand-watt smile, saying, "Yes, you are fit." Her smile turned pouty. "But you don't have any … padding."

When she skated around behind him, he whipped his head around so fast he almost tottered over. Folding her arms across her chest she said breathlessly, "Shane, I'd hate to see your body become a mass of bruises while you're learning." She rested a hand on the forearm he held out for balance. "I'll tell you what. I'll bring some hockey gear for you—it can help protect the more sensitive areas," she smiled with all her teeth and glanced up at him through her lashes, "and we'll see what you think. Okay?"

Chapter Four

Well at least he didn't have some eastern European old goat barking at him. Amelia Astor was pretty much what he had expected after reading her bio online and looking at a few pictures. She looked like Ike's idea of a foil. And her outfit? She wasn't doing herself any favors with black leggings and a shapeless, ratty fleece, which covered her to mid-thigh.

Her features were perfect. He could certainly see why the skating world had been whipped into a frenzy over her eight years ago, with her flawless skin and girl-next-door, fresh-scrubbed beauty. That pert, little nose, those wide-set, wholly vacant blue eyes, and masses and masses of thick, golden hair scraped back into a fat ponytail. Oh, she was beautiful—if you liked that soulless beauty queen look—and her chipper personality grated.

Learning a new skill was tough, and being instructed by this girl with her manic cheerleader mien added insult to injury. He didn't want or need her continual litany of platitudes or aggressive enthusiasm.

What was particularly irksome was how easy she made it look. He'd thought it would be a breeze. He was in the best shape of his life and had a knack for picking up everything from complicated dance choreography to surfing. But the ice was slick, the blades on the skates thin, and his ankles weak and unstable. There was not one thing easy about this sport, and it irritated the hell out of him. He'd been on the ice no more than ten minutes before he realized his athleticism wasn't going to help much. This was going to be work and more work, and take much longer than he'd anticipated. It was no wonder her rabid enthusiasm was getting on his nerves.

He'd seen pictures of her online from her youth and, lately, skating in the Enchanted show. Pictures of her smiling in her figure-hugging, tiny sequined dresses. It was a look reminiscent of the one he knew so well as an adolescent, dragged to his sister's beauty pageants. This woman was an Astor. Her father a descendant of one of the wealthiest families in America. Though only a thousand miles separated her birthplace in New York from his in Tennessee, she may as well have grown up in a different country for all he had in common with her.

His agent had done a masterful job of finding the type of woman who did not appeal to him. He'd expected to like her if only because she'd been described in her youth as a fierce competitor, her skating in her prime rapturously lauded as that rare combination of grace and athleticism.

According to the Internet, she'd been unflappable in contests, nailing even the most complicated triples. She'd put in enough flawless performances to be at the top of her game at the last competition before the Olympics—the Nationals. If there was criticism that kept popping up, it was a certain robotic feel to her skating, a lack of her own personality injected into her programs. After meeting her, he could understand that complaint—from what he could tell, she was about as deep as a puddle.

And then she'd up and quit. Right before the Olympics. Boom. Done. Over.

The great hope for Olympic medal glory quit to join an ice show. Hell, she was born into affluence and likely spoiled—maybe she wanted to be the center of attention in a different venue, or maybe she couldn't hack it. He slung his bag into the trunk.

He'd settled into the driver's seat when an assortment of motley vehicles began pulling into the lot. What was this? A hockey team arriving for practice? He studied the people piling out of the vehicles. There wasn't a single enforcer among them. And he would know, he'd spent a lot of time watching old hockey footage. He watched them enter the arena laughing and joking, one guy pulling a cooler. Was she safe in there? More cars filled the lot, a constant stream until at least a dozen people had made their way into the building.

Something wasn't right. And he'd left her in there.

Shane put his window down and turned off his car. He was about to open his door when Amy exited the building and skipped across the parking lot to a man chatting with two other guys next to the car one over from his. He scrunched down in the seat as she gave the tallest man a hug. The other two men greeted her before walking toward the building. So the princess had a boyfriend? The man wasn't much over six feet, but even from where he sat, Shane could see the musculature in the trim body.

"So who is the mystery man?" the guy said, his voice carrying in the sudden quiet of the parking lot.

"Shane Marx," Amy said.

He sucked in a breath.

So much for secrecy. Bitch. It would probably be everywhere tomorrow.

The man gave a low whistle. "You're teaching Shane Marx to skate?"

He gritted his teeth.

"Yep," she replied.

"I caught that movie he was in, the superhero thing. It was decent, but he was miscast."

Shane scowled.

The man continued, "What's he like?"

She mumbled something he couldn't quite catch, but whatever it was, the other man laughed. "That bad?"

He stiffened. Wait a minute. She was complaining about him?

She waved her hand dismissively and nodded. "Oh he's good-looking, but he's a grouch," she said.

Shane's mouth dropped open.

"You'll deal with it."

"And when you add that to his chronically on-the-make vibe, it's ... well, let's hope he's a quick learner and we can end this association sooner rather than later."

This was the woman who had spent the last hour training him? The perky, grinning debutante was badmouthing him? So he'd had a few fantasies about taking her up against the wall of the ice rink. He hadn't *said* he wanted to. And he hadn't realized he was so obvious. Clearly his initial assessment of her had been off.

The other man laughed heartily.

Who was this asshole? If his girlfriend was telling him this, why was he *laughing*?

"You really didn't like him," he said.

Amy sighed and took the man's hand, leading him away. "I don't know him, Kyle. So I'm going to see how this plays out. And I'm not going to let a personality clash get in the way of training. It's his money that's paying for rink time, so let's take advantage of it." He watched them enter the building.

That fact that they were using the facility on his dime was one thing, the fact that she couldn't keep her mouth shut was quite another. He pulled on his baseball hat and stalked toward the pulsating music and into the rink.

• • •

Sounds of a hip hop number with an infectious beat throbbed through him as he entered the cold arena. The rink was brightly lit, so he hugged the outer wall. He stood in the shadows, searching across the ice, then froze. There she was, in tight, black spandex—was that a tank top? Amy had taken off the ugly fleece, revealing well-defined arms and a decent, if small, rack. She was on the petite side—the top of her head would fit under his chin—but you could see the power in her legs and that tight ass. God, that ass. He groaned softly. He would've preferred if she'd kept that perfect, high, round bottom covered up. Now he would have trouble focusing no matter what she wore.

She was laughing with one of the guys—most of the men and women were lacing up skates, joking around. She left the side of the rink where she'd been chatting and started to skate. He pulled down his ball cap and hunched his shoulders; she glanced over, but in the shadows with his hair covered, she probably didn't get a good look.

Another song came on and she grinned—and it was quite a departure from the ferocious smiles she'd treated him to. She was completely in her element as she whirled around the rink at lightning speed. He watched dumbfounded. He knew this song, the summer's dirtiest hit. And there she was dancing to it, swinging that majestic booty. More skaters joined her on the ice. They had choreographed *this* song? It wasn't like they could perform it at a family ice show. This song was filthy and the skaters out on the ice were demonstrating moves that looked more like a striptease number than ice dancing. But it was … playful. They were laughing and having a great time out there.

He'd had days like this in TruAchord. Once they were all goofing off onstage before a show in some town somewhere—singing some nasty rap song and having a helluva time. Their manager reamed them out for risking their squeaky clean reputation. But those were the days before everyone had a recording device on their phone and their silliness would end up on YouTube, inciting outrage. They were allowed their harmless fun and a bonding experience with boys, not yet men, who were too often on the road.

Some of the skaters were still warming up, performing a few moves in synchronization, skating forward and backward with ease he envied, hooting and one-upping each other. Eventually Amy made her way over the rail near him, laughing so hard she was holding her side. He must've moved, for she peered into the shadows.

"Shane?" She mouthed his name, all traces of humor swept from her face.

He tugged the ball cap and took a dozen steps forward to meet her. She cast a furtive glance over her shoulder.

Her friend from the parking lot approached and Shane's jaw tightened.

"What are you still doing here?" she asked, her expression hard—all vestiges of the woman who had spent the hour training him gone.

He stared at her and saw what she'd masked before. Keen intelligence and irritation shone out of those thickly lashed blue eyes.

Her boyfriend came to a sudden stop, skates spitting ice shards at the rail.

"Shane, Kyle," she said by way of introduction. "Look, if you're trying to keep a low profile, this isn't the way to do it," she continued impatiently, making a shooing motion with her hand.

A few skaters glanced over but continued practicing their dance moves as the song changed to a seventies standard.

"I came in to remind you that if you can't keep your mouth shut about training me," he glanced at Kyle, who grinned, "we'll have a problem." He struggled to keep his tone even, but failed miserably.

Amy cocked her head and a furrow appeared between her brows, marring all that doll-like perfection.

"I'm not the one blowing your cover—" she began.

"I heard you tell him," he indicated Kyle with a jerk of his head, "in the parking lot."

Kyle's grin widened, but Amy cast a downward glance at the ice and rubbed her hand across her face. She was probably remembering what else she'd said.

She didn't even have the grace to look apologetic as her cool, disinterested gaze met his evenly.

"Kyle's my partner and he can keep his mouth shut. But if you value your anonymity, you'd best get the hell out of here before one of them," she jerked her head toward the ice, "gets a good look at you," she said, dismissing him with a backward glide.

He and Kyle exchanged a long look. But it was more of an assessment than a warning. A boyfriend who was her skating partner? He'd be surprised if that didn't spell disaster if his own experiences playing where he worked were anything to go by.

"*Ciao*," Kyle said, also skating backward, still smiling like a fool.

Shane grunted and stepped back into the shadows. He stayed another hour to watch, barely able to keep his eyes off Amy's black clad body. He'd been with women in seriously good shape but this woman … her spins and leaps out on the slick surface blew him away. Like her or not, she was fucking awesome.

Chapter Five

Amy waited outside the rink the following evening. She checked her watch again. Damn it, he was fifteen minutes late. If she wasn't careful, her friends would be bumping into him when the lesson ended. Maybe she could lock the front door and send him out the back? Her stomach twisted with irritation.

Finally, she heard the growl of an expensive engine, and his silver fancy car turned into the lot.

He strode over, bag in hand, and she scowled at him—she'd taken the gloves off last night and they weren't going back on.

"You're late."

He shrugged.

She put her hands on her hips, blocking his access to the front doors. "My time is valuable, so don't be late again or you won't find me here waiting."

He laughed, but it was humorless. "Oh, you'll be waiting. You need the rink time for your friends."

She backed up a step and he brushed by her into the building.

Amy stalked after him. "Listen, Shane."

He stopped and turned around. "You listen. You're using my money to have your friends work out. Let them pay for their own rink time."

She stared at him. "There's a minimum rink rental of three hours, I don't think—"

"Then I'll use what I pay for."

Oh he would? Skate for three hours? *We'll see about that.*

"Fine. Get your skates on." She turned away to send a group text, letting her friends from Enchanted know they wouldn't get rink time tonight. Only eight were able to make it anyway, since most of them worked weekend nights wherever they could during the summer when the show was on hiatus.

He wanted a three-hour workout, he'd get one. He may not be able to walk tomorrow, but she'd give him his money's worth and then some.

• • •

Shane lost count of how many times he'd fallen, but he knew he'd be sporting a spectacular collection of bruises tomorrow. He staggered to his feet and met the slave driver's eyes. Her expression registered begrudging respect—or maybe sympathy—before her features resettled themselves into bland disinterest. She held out a hand to help him to his feet. He ignored it, rising slowly, painfully. His ankles screamed in agony, his legs, limp noodles.

Four days a week, Marco, his personal trainer, put him through two hours of weights and cardio at the gym. And since he hadn't worked in nearly a year, Shane ran, swam, or surfed when he felt like it, which was most days. For a guy in such great shape, this ice skating was kicking his butt. His life had fallen into a pattern of workouts, script reading, lunches with friends, or time at the pool or beach. He was bored and he hated the roles he was offered, the lightweight love interest, the nice guy next door. The role of Hank LaMott, washed up hockey player making a mess of his life and the lives of everyone around him was perfect for him. What's more, it could forever change the way Hollywood viewed Shane Marx.

Now that he knew the audition was coming, he had to bulk up a bit. Twenty pounds would align his body with the role.

He'd forced himself to stay out of the clubs the last few weeks, but the abstinence was getting to him. Between the evening skating lessons and fears of another busted condom, he hadn't been out trolling since the incident.

Horny and irritable, he watched Amy shrug and skate away, a graceful glide across the ice. He may loathe her, but he still wanted to tap that. Thirty minutes and two falls later he was ready to call it when she said, "Okay, we're done for tonight."

Shane closed his eyes with relief.

"Are you all right?" she asked.

"Fine," he bit out. His second lesson and he had the forward glide down—no more of that penguin stepping bullshit. The backward skating was more difficult, but he was pleased with his progress, and judging by Amy's encouragement, she was satisfied also.

She sat next to him on the bench, unlacing her skates.

He bit back a groan of relief as he pulled one foot out of the skate. Rubbing his left foot, he turned and met her gaze.

She slipped on her Ugg boots and pulled her hair out of its bun, giving it a shake and sending the scent of coconut and vanilla wafting over.

His groin tightened as lust thickened his blood. He needed to get laid. Well, after he pulled on his shoes.

She stood with her bag, dangling the keys to the rink in her hand.

He levered himself to his feet, his legs shaking. He reached for something to steady himself, and the nearest object was Amy, so he grabbed her shoulder. She shifted her weight to accommodate him.

God, what he wouldn't give to bury himself in all that tropical scent. To have that head bobbing down on his throbbing cock, to be watching that shiny, golden head—

He grunted and moved his arm away, finding his balance on trembling legs.

The ice princess bit her lip.

Shane's gaze tracked the small, perfect teeth teasing the plump, bow-shaped lip, and he moved his skate bag to cover his swelling erection. Too bad his cock hadn't gotten the message his legs were sending. He could barely stand, let alone screw.

"Do you need help?" she asked, guilt sketched into her features.

"Nah," he said, shuffling toward the exit.

She trailed him, locking the door behind them before she made her way to her beat-up silver Miata.

"Shane?" she called over to him.

He unlocked his car door. "What?"

"Try ibuprofen and a hot shower. A massage might help, too. Tomorrow, do a light workout to get the lactic acid out of the muscles, okay?"

"Yeah." He groaned as he slid into the low-slung car, his legs shaking so hard his knees were practically knocking together. Muscles and bruises protested as he settled himself into the seat. If it sucked this bad now, he could only imagine how much tomorrow and the day after would blow.

Chapter Six

Amy wandered to the window where she got the best cell reception in the house and stared across the street at the forty-foot high palm trees in desperate need of trimming. She'd heard rats made nests in them when they weren't cared for. This was the sketchier side of Westwood, and no one in this part of town would be grooming the palm trees. The neighborhood, like the tiny three-bedroom house, was run down but affordable and relatively safe. It was the kind of area that rented month-to-month houses and ugly garden apartments without pools, a temporary home for veteran skaters like her, Kyle, and Allyson between stints on the road. Not the kind of place Astors inhabited, but then she hadn't been an Astor since she'd left that world behind at seventeen.

She'd been dreading making this call. Would he complain about how sore he was? He'd earned her begrudging respect after that skating lesson yesterday, but if she pushed him too hard, he'd injure himself. Then it would be good-bye twenty-thousand dollars and the end of her chance to be spotted before Enchanted made up their mind about casting. She'd tell him practice was canceled and suggest meeting for coffee in Brentwood—somewhere trendy where they could be seen together. This was what Kyle had been leaning on her to do. She'd tried explaining their mutual dislike to him, to no avail. "If you want Enchanted, Amy, generate some interest, the clock is ticking," he'd said.

He answered on the first ring, his husky baritone sending a tingle down her spine.

"Hey, Shane. Listen, the rink is tied up with an event tonight. Some scheduling snafu. Frank was very apologetic. We'll pick it up again tomorrow, okay?" Amy pressed the phone against her ear with her shoulder.

"No problem. Uh ... would you want to grab a drink or something?" he said.

She hesitated. "I guess." He'd beaten her to it. Why?

"Spoke?" Shane said.

"Spoke?" she echoed. Not exactly a low profile place. Or so she'd heard. She didn't frequent ultra-hip rooftop terrace bars with fire pits and pools where a martini cost twice as much as her standard meal out.

"I'll pick you up. How does six work for you?"

"Fine, but aren't you concerned about ... well, about people figuring it out?"

"Nah. My agent's already put it out there that I'm a skater. It can't hurt for the producers to think I'm good enough for your august company."

"We're still keeping quiet about our training?"

"Yeah." There was a long pause. "I'm up for a role, and they think I know how to ice skate. It's not a complete lie anymore. I figure since we had the time booked, I'd like to get to know you. I really appreciate your help and I feel like we got off on the wrong foot," he said, smoothly.

She hung up the phone. Spoke would be the perfect place. Was he sincere about appreciating her help? She could not bring herself to like him. Initially she had wanted to keep her distance, especially given his reputation as a womanizer. The looks he gave her body could melt ice, but he wasn't flirtatious. Far from it. Chilly professionalism best described their relationship since that first meeting.

She rifled through her closet, looking for that right combination. Here was an opportunity to dress the Amelia Astor part and hope someone noticed them at Spoke. And that someone at Enchanted was paying attention, too. Unfortunately, she didn't have anything appropriately trendy enough for Spoke.

But Allyson, her roommate, would and when it came to clothing, Allyson pulled out all the stops.

He roared up in a sports car—a red convertible one this time and only ten minutes late. She climbed in the beige leather passenger's seat and caught his wary look. "What?"

"Used to seeing you in workout attire."

She shrugged. "You should see me in full makeup and princess regalia."

They made small talk about the latest Lee Child thriller and argued good-naturedly about casting decisions made for the movie. Twenty minutes later, Shane pulled alongside the curb of an art deco building in Santa Monica. He gave the car keys to a valet and came around to help her out of the car. They took the elevator to the rooftop, and with a nod at the sentry, they passed through the final door to the patio. It was just past seven and the sky was still bright, so they found seating on a couch near a fire pit in a little cabana area complete with tied back curtains. What did people do up here that warranted closing the curtains? Drugs? Sex?

She sat on the plush, black cushion, skirmishing with her hem for the millionth time. She never would have borrowed Allyson's stupid dress if she'd know she'd be battling exposure every time she sat down. The ridiculous strapless thing that looked so cute on a hanger had to be either tugged up to keep her breasts covered or pulled down to keep her booty covered—but was incapable of handling both jobs simultaneously. Clearly it was not designed for someone with breasts, hips, or a skater's full butt. She draped her wrap over her bag, tempted to use it to cover her legs, as Shane's gaze drifted over her body again.

A waitress with a gleaming smile and a very short, navy skirt came over to take their order. Shane gave her the once over, too, and he must've liked what he saw because he went from distant to flirtatious in two heartbeats. He chatted with her about Spoke, and when she leaned over to point to a few items on the drink menu, Shane appeared more interested in what was coming out of her top than in the leather bound booklet. Amy watched, disgusted.

She must have been a little too obvious because the waitress cast a couple of nervous glances in her direction.

Amy hid her irritation with a frozen smile.

When the woman walked away, Shane commented, "So, something I've been meaning to ask you. I know you've probably been asked this before … "

Only a million freakin' times.

"Why did you leave competition? You were at the top of the skating world when you quit—"

"Why did you leave music for acting?"

Shane shifted on the couch, met her eyes, and shrugged.

She shrugged in return. If she didn't need to be seen with him, she would've ditched him over the heavy eye contact and ogling the waitress. What kind of guy did that when out with another woman?

He'd earned a bit of respect completing her two-and-a-half-hour skating torture the other night, but knowing him, that determination was a character flaw, too—she could add stubborn and unreasonable to her litany of complaints.

She'd developed an unhealthy fascination with Shane Marx. After her first lesson she'd dug up all there was to know about the guy—that he'd been with TruAchord for five years, until the band disintegrated thanks to infighting, rehab, and egos. Some of the band members had dropped off the face of the earth, a few had gone on to do television or commercials. Shane, with his looks, had walked from one successful venture directly into another: Hollywood, with barely a misstep. That is, until the last few years, when the stories had started to come out. Vengeful ex-girlfriends who went public about infidelities, difficulties with female co-stars and crew, naked photos.

"Acting was a natural progression. Leaving a sport where you are nationally ranked on your way to Olympic glory for an ice show is whacked," he said when she continued to ignore him.

He had no tact, not one shred.

Most thought it. No one ever said it to her face.

"Maybe the circuit was whacked?" *Or my life on the circuit.*

He lifted his brows. "And the shows aren't?"

She met his gaze, those blue eyes that missed little, a stare that had graced the covers of any number of entertainment magazines in the last decade. She hadn't made the mistake of underestimating his intelligence or his drive. Clearly he had both in spades. She still didn't have any clue why he'd invited her out, but it wasn't about gratitude or interest, considering all the heavy innuendo with the damn waitress.

The woman came back, caught Amy's stink eye, dropped off the drinks, and departed hastily.

"Not Enchanted. Others, maybe."

"I'm sorry, what?" he said absently as he watched the waitress hustle away.

God! What an asshole.

She sucked down most of her drink in two swallows and examined the glass. That was a damned good martini. It made her regret her two-martini limit.

He turned back to face her, giving her his attention. "Why are you still doing it—the princess thing? Hasn't it gotten old?"

"No. And it's not like I have a gazillion career options."

"Why not coach?"

She set her glass carefully on the table, her head swimming. That was a strong drink on an empty stomach. She needed to eat, stat, before she got really loopy. She glanced around for the waitress, knowing they'd be lucky to get her back.

"Another?" He raised an eyebrow at her glass.

"An appetizer would be good about now."

He handed her the sheet of paper listing specials. She selected a sushi entrée, Shane flagged the woman down, and ordered food and another round.

"So, no coaching?"

Amy narrowed her eyes and shook her head. Would he just drop it already?

"Why not? Seems like something retired skaters do."

Retired. She stifled a shudder, put her shoulders back, and re-crossed her legs. "I'm not ready to retire."

"When do you go back out on the road?" Shane turned toward her and laid an arm on the back of the couch, his fingers close enough to brush her hair. Faded denim stretched tightly across his muscular thighs. She dragged her gaze from his lap to meet his knowing smile.

Amy smoothed her hair out of her face, the material across her breasts slipping until her nipples were nearly exposed. She sat on her hands to prevent herself from yanking it up. A hungry expression wiped the half smile from his face and darkened his eyes to navy.

Do I have your attention now?

"Not sure," she mumbled. Now that she had his interest, she wasn't sure she wanted it. All that intensity channeled into lust was highly arousing. Her hormones were raging and his body … that stupid, fucking picture she'd looked at, then looked at again.

That had been a mistake. The damn image popped into her head when they were skating, talking, last thing at night, first thing in the morning. Days they trained, days they didn't. Is this what guys went through when they met a Playmate? Did they have trouble focusing or were they continually thinking about what the other person looked like unclothed?

Was it really him? What she wouldn't give to know that story.

She couldn't remember a time when she'd wanted a guy so desperately. Wanted to rip off his clothes and lick him from head to toe.

It was confusing to be hot for someone she couldn't stand.

"Have you been picked up for this season?" he was saying.

Amy glanced around the quiet terrace. "Hmmm?" she said, with studied casualness. "Picked up? It's not like the NFL draft. I've been a *principal* with them for years."

He watched her intently, eyebrows raised, not buying it. "They *haven't* signed you though, have they?"

"They will," she said, giving her hair another toss. After being seen with Shane Marx. A photo or two splashed on the Internet, a renewed interest in her past would be all it took to have Enchanted begging her to re-sign for another season. They could use the press. Ticket sales had dropped off in the last few years, but the Olympics weren't far off and someone always rehashed her story around that time—this was the first year she'd be grateful for it.

He gave a shout of laughter and she frowned at him.

"What?" she said.

"Am I being played here?"

"I'm not going to try to take naked photos, if that's what you're asking." She took another sip. "That wouldn't have the intended effect on my career." This drink was dangerously smooth, lovely.

He ignored the dig. "Why did you agree to go out with me?"

"You're hot," she said, playing with a strand of hair, blinking up at him with her best princess smile. Her smile faltered as she moved forward imperceptibly, out of the reach of those long fingers.

"I think you're here with me for the same reason I'm with you."

Amy affixed her best wide-eyed, innocent expression—her face fell naturally into those lines. "Attraction?"

She resisted the urge to yank up the dress again and tried to take shallow breaths.

"Publicity," he retorted.

She stilled. "Is *that* why you asked me out?" she said, almost inaudibly.

"My agent encouraged it. He's in the throes of panic over my image," he stated.

His Ike.

Her Kyle.

"Right. He's the one who set up the … " she glanced around furtively, "lessons."

"I need the lessons, obviously, but he's trying to kill two birds with one stone here." Shane gestured between them.

So he was using her the same way she was using him. That was fair. Then why was she so disgruntled?

"Why me?"

"You have to ask? Amelia Astor, princess, New England blue-blood. Incorruptible. You're the ideal woman to rehab my image—according to Ike—and he's never wrong about crap like that, so here we are."

That stung. It was the way he said it. As though he would never in a million years be seen with her otherwise.

"And here *you* are just in time to resuscitate my contract." She raised her glass. "Cheers," she said, without the slightest bit of pique reflected in her tone.

He gave her a genuine smile and clinked her glass. "Cheers."

Amy forced a laugh. "A fictitious relationship to aid our careers? How pathetic."

"How LA," he responded drily.

Goaded, she stretched out a hand and laid it, palm down on his rock hard, jean clad thigh, one finger tracing a pattern on the soft cotton. She leaned in, smiling smugly as his gaze dropped to her breasts, and whispered, "I'm not incorruptible."

He tilted his head back, and she watched his throat work as he finished his drink in one swallow and scooted closer. "No?"

She whipped her hand away, before it ended up at the seam of his crotch.

"It doesn't *have* to be fiction, but I don't do fidelity," he said as his long fingers tucked a strand of her blonde hair behind her ear and he shot her a half-smile that sent a throb of excitement through her traitorous body.

She shifted on the couch.

"Ike got me what I wanted, and now I'm doing this for him. He's trying to get me back in the good graces of certain producers. After all the crap that's come down the past two years, I recently lost my first audition."

"Sorry to hear that," she murmured.

"I didn't want it anyway."

"No?" Amy feigned interest. This was the part where he went on and on about acting. She'd been out with her share of actors during summers in Hollywood. Usually they were waiter/actors, but nonetheless, she'd heard more about the business than she cared to in her lifetime.

"No. I'm done with all that. I'm only taking roles that speak to me."

She pressed her lips together and widened her eyes. "Is there a Charlie Sheen biopic casting?"

His eyebrows shot up, then he laughed. "That came out wrong. Jesus, being in Hollywood all this time you start *talking* like them. I never used to sound like this. Like some jackass talking about the 'craft' or whatever. And then the press has a field day with every little thing."

"You have gotten some bad press." She managed to keep her tone neutral.

He looked around the terrace, avoiding her gaze. "It's the nature of this town. Everything is fair game and the women. . ." His voice trailed off and an expression of revulsion crossed his face.

"Oh, the *women* are the problem?" This time she couldn't keep the skepticism out of her voice. From what she'd read online, the fact that he couldn't keep his hands off his co-stars was the problem.

Shane waved a hand. "They have to document everything on social media, brag to their friends. Gone are the days when you could get off with someone and go your separate ways. Now people post photos and tweet—everyone in the public eye gets burned, not only me. It used to be the paparazzi were the ones you had to avoid. Now it's everyone with a phone—so basically everyone." He ran a hand through his hair.

Amy took another sip of her drink and realized she'd finished it. Damn. And his wasn't even half gone. She better slow down or she'd be smashed. Where was the food?

"I get in these situations and … stuff happens. Whatever."

"I imagine it sucks to have naked pictures out there."

He studied her through curious eyes.

The heat rose in her face. She must be drunk if she was bringing up that subject.

"Picture."

"What?"

"*A* naked picture."

"Yeah. That."

His hand slid into her hair at the nape of her neck and stroked. "That's the second reference you've made to that picture of my cock. Curious?"

She couldn't suppress a full body shiver or the throb coming to life at his words. "No," she lied huskily.

He scooted closer.

Everything in Amy was poised for retreat—but Amelia sprung to life, meeting and holding his gaze.

His expression was bland, but his breath sawed in and out of his body. He might make her shiver, but she made him pant, she realized with satisfaction.

Take that, waitress.

49

She must be more buzzed than she thought. And there was something about this guy that brought out every competitive instinct she'd ever had. It wasn't like men fell all over themselves to be with her, but the lack of interest this one exhibited was galling.

Shane's gaze was glued to the front of her dress. She took a deep breath and the dress slipped, exposing a sliver of her left areola. The intensity in his gaze seared through her, triggering her thighs to clench together in an attempt to stifle the pulsating ache between them.

His warm fingers left her nape to thread through her hair, and with an ungentle grip, he pulled her head toward his.

Arousal churned though her, leaving her lightheaded with desire. Acquiescent, she moved toward him, immobilized by the heat in the depths of his azure eyes, the lust etched into the sharp planes of his face. Amy closed her eyes.

He laved her lower lip with his tongue and her mouth parted on a gasp, her hand tightening involuntarily on his upper thigh.

He maneuvered her head, stroking his lips leisurely against hers, teasing.

She pressed her hips into the cushion of the patio sofa in a fruitless attempt to slake the desperate, empty aching. She arched toward him, vaguely aware the uncooperative dress was releasing itself of its obligation to cover her chest as she contorted her body to fit against his.

Her hand stole around his neck, gripping the broad column, urging him on.

His wide chest pressed her further into the cushions as his slick tongue swept inside her mouth, the hand on the back of her head tightening in her hair until it was almost painful, and she moaned into his mouth. He lifted one of her legs over his. She inhaled his exotic scent, tasted the tang of the gin on his breath. He deepened the kiss, his tongue stroking, tangling with hers, as his wide palm met her bare thigh.

God, yes.

Her legs parted, instinctively, craving his touch. She squirmed against him and his hand slid higher.

She held his mouth to her with two hands now wrapped in his thick hair, mindless as her lips explored the rough texture of his cheek and jaw before finding the surprising softness of his lips.

His fingers reached the satin barrier of her soaked panties and he made a sound—surprise? Pleasure? He cupped her and she writhed, his mouth capturing her gasp of pleasure as his two fingers slipped inside the waistband of her thong and found her slick seam.

Oh God, she was so close—

What the fuck?

Leaning back she broke contact with his lips with a grunt. Her hand left his neck to grip his wrist and she pulled his hand out of her panties, away from her desperate body.

Inches apart they panted, never breaking eye contact.

Amy released his hand and scooted away, her body still throbbing, aching for completion. Instead, she hitched up the dress.

Shane sat up and glanced over at the curtains pulled back around their little patio with couch and coffee table. He leaned sideways to finger the tassel holding the curtains open, looking over at her in askance.

She gave a shaky laugh, struggling for composure. "Whatever you're thinking, no. For so many reasons, no. We're here to *improve* your image, remember? Ike would have you blackballed. And I'm trying to win back my role as a princess in a family show, not show up on TMZ in a sex tape. "

She wriggled still farther away, until she was well out of reach of those hands.

What the hell was that?

A waiter appeared so suddenly with their food, Amy realized he must have been watching them.

"Want to get out of here then?" he asked, still staring at her, ignoring the plate of tapas and sushi.

"No. No I don't. That was ... well, you know—"

"For public consumption?" He glanced around the quiet rooftop. "We may want to hang out a while and try again or go somewhere else, since no one but our waiter seemed to notice us tucked back here behind the planters."

He noticed who had been noticing? Or not noticing. God. She had been on the verge of orgasm thanks to those skilled fingers, while he had maintained a level of awareness. There was something about the way he smelled. And his body—and all that focused intensity. This attraction was a complication she did not need. Not if she hoped to continue to coach him.

Chapter Seven

Three weeks after Ike's infamous call Amy lay in bed the morning after another grueling practice. Crossovers were challenging for a new skater, but they were critical for Shane's hockey role. Why was he being so stubborn about the pads? He had to be a mass of bruises after all those falls, and the last thing she needed was a delay in their schedule because he got hurt. She needed the money from this job to last the rest of the summer and maybe beyond.

Something shifted in their relationship that night at Spoke—there was less hostility. That kiss had been a mistake of epic proportions, because she now looked forward to their lessons like a giddy fan girl, though she had too much pride to let him see how he affected her.

She still wouldn't describe him as friendly, but he was less guarded and noticeably more relaxed. She pictured him that night at Spoke, his hand stroking her, his tongue ravaging her, and the memory sent a throb through her. Amy closed her eyes and her hand drifted down under the sheets, trailing its way to the juncture of her thighs, remembering the taste of his mouth, his hardness under the cotton jeans—

Her phone rang.

Shane's ringtone.

She coughed to clear the sleep and arousal out of her voice before answering.

"You want to go to La Croix for lunch?" he asked.

"Uh," she hesitated, glancing at the clock. "I was planning to go for a run this morning."

"Oh yeah? I could use a workout. Where do you go?"

"Will Rogers Beach—I go on the bike path to Santa Monica and back."

"You don't run on the beach?"

"No," she hesitated. "I can't. It's too hard on my hip."

"You're injured?" he asked, surprise registering in his tone.

"No, it's more like a chronic thing. Sand is not my friend; I'm better on flat surfaces."

"Not a problem. Bike path it is then. Eleven at the lifeguard headquarters?"

"Okay," she said slowly.

He hung up and Amy stared at the phone. They hadn't said anything about pace or distance. What if he was some running fiend and she couldn't keep up? Why did she agree to this? She liked to run to her music, not gasp out a conversation.

Forty-five minutes later she parked her Miata at the beach. She saw Shane in an ancient, faded Reeking Bliss t-shirt and navy athletic shorts, leaning his hand up against the lifeguard building, stretching his quads. She gaped at the musculature in his legs. No wonder he was making such strides skating—he was rock solid everywhere.

Get a grip, Amy.

He raised his arms over his head and the t-shirt rose, revealing such perfectly sculpted abdominal muscles she felt vaguely intimidated. Her eyes tracked the narrow trail of hair that disappeared into his waistband and she felt the heat rise in her face. Locking the car, she made her way over to him.

Hopefully he didn't view this run as some payback for all the times she'd tortured him on the ice.

He nodded at her and without a word, she tucked her key into the arm pocket of her running top and took off down the path. It was on.

Shane loped easily next to her.

She glanced over. "What's your pace?"

He shrugged and shot her a grin. "Whatever."

They ran in silence next to the Pacific, passing or being passed by the occasional cyclist, Rollerblader, or runner.

Every so often, she picked up her pace. With a knowing glance, he matched her stride for stride.

Good. He didn't want to chat. After the first thirty minutes, she didn't think she could get out two words anyway. And despite the fact that she usually finished her six-mile runs at a good pace, clearly she was outclassed. He hadn't broken a sweat, while she was sweating profusely and wondering if she'd make it back to the car.

She spotted the guy on the purple beach cruiser bike a ways off. Typical SoCal beach kid—shirtless with board-shorts, he approached them at a good clip on the opposite side of the path.

Suddenly the guy veered into their lane. Shane shouted, "Watch out!" but the dude was wearing earbuds and messing with his phone, so he didn't hear or see them.

With dawning horror Amy slowed, but she was directly in his path, the momentum from her stride carrying her forward.

She couldn't get out of the way.

"Fuck," Shane bit out.

She'd just put her hands up to brace for the impact when she felt a brutal shove, hard enough to send her tumbling onto the sandy grass area next to the path and out of harm's way. Rolling to her back, she looked up in time to see the Shane go down with the rider in a twisted mix of limbs and metal.

She picked herself up and stumbled over to where the two men lay, the bicycle a few feet away.

"Shane? Oh my God, Shane. Are you okay? She went to her knees beside him, helping him up with an arm around his shoulders. He sat up with a groan, holding his head.

Her hand swept over him, but other than some road rash on his arm, she couldn't see any injuries.

Shane shook his arms out experimentally, moved his legs, and got his feet gingerly. The texting idiot was still lying on the ground.

Two senior citizens in sweat suits hurried over.

"Oh my goodness, is everyone okay?" one of the women asked. Shane didn't answer but dragged the bike out of the path.

The young guy got to his feet slowly, grunting and cursing, his chest scratched and bleeding from the impact with the asphalt. He touched himself and winced.

"Where's my phone?" he said, looking up at them.

Amy spied it in the grass but said nothing.

"What the hell, man?" Shane spat out.

"What?" he retorted. "You ran in to me."

Shane shook his head, then had to steady himself on her shoulder. "Give me a minute. My head took a good bounce," he said.

"Maybe we should get to a hospital. It could be a concussion."

"Nah. I'll be fine."

"Thanks for knocking me out of the way," she said, awed as she watched him recover his bearings. He had to know he'd take a hit for her. The bike was headed straight for her.

"Where's my fucking phone?" the guy said again, scowling at them as he picked up his bike.

Amy's mouth dropped open. "You have got to be kidding me. You crashed into him because you were messing with your phone. You're a menace," she hissed.

"You ran into me," the kid insisted.

"No," the older woman piped up, "you weren't looking and crossed over the line into them. We saw the whole thing. You almost mowed us down, too. I have half a mind to call the police."

Clearly the guy didn't like that idea. He grabbed his bike, warped front tire and all, and took off down the bike path.

She bit her lip. They were more than a mile from the parking lot and there was no way Shane should be driving. How hard did he hit his head? She'd seen her share of skaters with concussions who also seemed fine right after the accident. She didn't like to take chances. "Hey," she said to the more vocal of the two witnesses, "do you mind keeping an eye on him while I get my car?"

"I'm fine, Amy," Shane insisted, taking a step forward.

All the women ignored him.

"We'd be happy to," the woman in the green tracksuit said. She gave Shane a mischievous look. "Don't make me sit on you, young man."

"I'll be back," Amy said, taking off down the path.

• • •

Hours after dropping Shane off at his Santa Monica condo and calling twice to check on him, Amy entered O'Hooligans, searching the dim interior for Kyle.

"Hey, got your text that you rescheduled practice," Kyle said as she scooted across the booth.

"I gave him the night off and traded time with Frank. This morning when we were running down the path, Shane got mowed down by a cyclist. He shoved me out of the way and took the hit."

"He okay?"

"Yeah." She nursed the pint of lager Kyle had already ordered for her.

"So what's bugging you?" he asked patiently. They only had an hour before the rest of the crew met them. "You're shredding napkins and that's always a bad sign."

"Shane."

"Uh huh."

"Don't sound so smug."

Kyle leaned back and studied her, his expression deceptively lazy.

"I had him pigeonholed, you know? That he's selfish and arrogant. But he has the intensity of a professional athlete when it comes to our workouts. And after what happened this morning … " she trailed off.

"So chivalry isn't quite dead."

Amy toyed with the remnants of the napkins, pilling them. "Shane risked serious injury for me."

"I'm still not getting how he managed shove you out of the way and not get out of the way himself."

"It happened so fast," she said, staring into space. "One minute the asshole was in his own lane, looking at his cell—the next he was coming right at *me*. Shane could've gotten out of the way. I think most people would try to save themselves, you know?"

"It would've been my first instinct."

Kyle reached across the table and covered her hand that was still destroying the napkin. "One selfless act doesn't make him a good guy."

Amy cocked her head and leveled at look at him. "No?"

Kyle groaned and grabbed his beer. "Why do women always do this?"

"Do what?"

"Read too much into some random thing. Look so hard for the good in someone; they miss all the red flags. Why do you all always want to fix the damage?"

"Is that what I'm doing?"

He nodded. "You don't have to make him into something he's not because you want to sleep with him."

Amy made a sound of protest.

Kyle laughed. "Don't bother denying it. I know the signs. Why can't you revel in the bad and have fun with it? The guy's an actor for Chrissakes. He was in a band. He's good-looking, successful, and loaded. Any one of those experiences would fuck someone up—but all of it combined? His ego *cannot* be healthy. Look at his rep, Amy. You know what Enchanted's set designer Marisa said happened on his film she worked on two summers ago? He played three women against each other and the picture almost went down in flames."

She could believe it. Shane Marx was arrogant and tactless and a womanizer. She'd seen all of those things for herself. He was also intense, competitive and chivalrous.

He'd shoved her out of the path of that bicycle, putting himself at risk.

Maybe she *was* trying to rationalize her attraction to him.

Amy took another sip of beer while Kyle scanned the darkened room for the waiter. Service was terrible in this place but the food was good, the beer was cheap, and the darts were free.

• • •

Amy climbed out of the shower a few days later after an early morning run. She finally had a day off. The rescheduled day last week after Shane's run in with the bike had turned into two days hiatus and they'd had five days in a row of intense skating work-outs. She was ridiculously proud of his progress, but was well aware it wasn't some heretofore unknown coaching skill. The guy was a quick study and a hard worker. She combed through her hair. She finally had time to catch up on laundry and grocery shopping but she didn't want to do any of that. The hand holding the brush froze in midair. She wanted to see him. Was she bummed because she wouldn't see him today?

Putting the brush down, she yanked off the towel, hung it on the rack and went to dress. No. That couldn't be it. She just didn't want to spend the day doing all the chores that had piled up.

She had just poured her second cup of coffee when her phone rang.

Her pulse pounded. *Shane.*

"Hello?"

"Can I pick you up at noon for lunch? And dress the part, would you? Ike was scandalized by that outfit you wore to Spoke."

"Ike? Does that mean—"

The call disconnected before Amy could finish her thought. She made a sound, a cross between a snort and groan, and stared at the phone in her hand. How had Ike known what she was wearing? Were they outed online already? Heart in her throat, she raced over to her laptop and Googled herself. Nope. Nothing new and she didn't have time to scroll through a million pages of images of Shane. She didn't want to encounter that naked picture of him. Not again. She'd looked at that damn picture so many times it was imprinted on her brain.

If she'd been seen with him, Enchanted would have called.

She frowned. Who did he think he was, dictating her attire? No wonder he had trouble with women.

She needed to draw a little more attention to herself. Not for Shane's sake, but to get noticed around town. That trumped any of his orders. Amy knocked on her roommate Allyson's door.

"Allyson? Can I borrow something to wear?" Her friend looked up from her laptop and grunted, indicating her closet.

Thirty minutes later she examined her outfit in the full-length mirror in the hall. She walked through to the living room where Kyle was stretched out on the couch, recovering from a late night or early morning. His mouth dropped open when he saw her. "Holy shit, Amy."

She gave him her wide-eyed innocent expression.

"Ugh. Don't give me that look. It's creepy with that getup." He sat up, taking in her micro-mini plaid skirt, white Peter Pan collared shirt, and black boots. "You're rockin' that school girl outfit."

If Kyle Reed thought her attire was overkill, it probably was. With a sigh she slid a button through another button hole, grabbed a modest cardigan, and returned to the living room.

"Good look, Amy, what's the occasion? You moonlighting over at Chicks on Dix?"

Through the window she saw Shane's car turn into the driveway.

Kyle's puzzled expression turned gleeful. "Shane?"

"Yep."

He shook his head. "My, my Amy, so competitive. I couldn't make a bet on who will come out on top with this one, but I'll betcha someone does." He laughed at his own joke.

"*Suck it*, Kyle."

She slammed the door almost loud enough not to hear his "you will" response.

• • •

Shane watched with disbelieving eyes as Amy hustled down the walkway, three inches taller in her boots, and climbed into the waiting car. That was the tiniest skirt he'd seen. And he was a micro-mini connoisseur.

He stared at her for a moment as she settled herself on the seat next to him, then roared away from the curb.

At the light he looked over at her. "I guess I wasn't clear on Ike's expectations."

She turned in her seat and the too small cotton blouse lifted, displaying a sliver of tan midriff and triggering insta-lust. He lifted his gaze back to her face, recognizing the defiance in those jewel-like blue eyes.

"Oh, you were clear. But you might want to tell your agent that I only *play* an innocent princess. And no one dictates my look. Not unless I'm on the ice and you have a contract with me. I have news for you and your manager: I'm *not* innocent. No one stays innocent on the road. I've seen or heard about everything," she said, hotly. "And I have my own agenda. Remember? This could get the attention we both need." She tugged the hemline.

But he ignored that, focusing on the other comment. "Seen everything, huh?" He highly doubted that. It wasn't just how she looked, all dewy-eyed innocence. She performed in a children's ice show. How depraved could that be? Then again, none of them had maintained their innocence once TruAchord toured.

She waved a hand. "I've had the good fortune to be propositioned here and abroad, even through hand gestures in foreign countries."

"Sex?"

She moved her hand dismissively as he negotiated the traffic. He'd take her to his favorite little taqueria where no one would bat an eye at her attire. Being seen with him, dressed as she was, would not persuade Enchanted to sign her. He may not know skating, but he knew the reputation of the company who employed her. They were well known in the television and film industry for their conservatism. There had been shakeups over the years and they'd modernized, but they were never happy when one of their starlets—or princesses—went rogue. He couldn't have Amy perceived as going over to the dark side. For this to work, she needed to be seen dragging him into the light.

She needed to be the Enchanted princess, not girl gone wild. Cafe Ta—the latest hangout for the reality show starlets and those of that ilk—might do the trick. After practice when she was at her fresh scrubbed, casual best. Their fictitious relationship needed to be perceived as PG, not NC-17. Clearly she was desperate to rejoin the cast in the fall but didn't have the first idea about how the game was played, or what his reputation could do to hers solely via association.

He tuned in to hear her complain, "Playing a princess brings out the worst in grown men. What is it with the naïve girl thing? I'm continually offered money for my virginity! As *if*. That ship sailed long ago," she said.

He pulled the car over to the curb in front of the Mexican place, turned it off, and stared at her. Then he burst out laughing. "Good God, Amy. Really?"

She cocked her head and gave him a considering look. "I can identify weirdos in five seconds. You have your issues, but you aren't fetishy, are you?"

"No. My tastes are pretty pedestrian—the normal kink. And what do you mean 'issues'?"

She ignored the question. "Women don't ask *you* for sex fantasy things?"

He shrugged, looking away. "Nothing I'd consider odd."

"Really?"

"I've never been offered money for sex. Singing? Yeah. Commercials, bar mitzvahs, Sweet Sixteen parties, you name it. I've sold out a hundred times over. They don't always pay me the big bucks to act, but I can still make a bundle singing for private parties. I don't perform much anymore, but some of my old band mates do. Sex? I wish."

She cocked her head, considering him. "After shows sometimes men come to the dressing room. You've had that, right? Women coming in after shows?"

He nodded, keeping his expression closed.

"They tip security or whoever. They make … requests. Normal stuff. Deviant stuff. And it's not unique to this country. I'm some kind of a magnet … well, not me, but 'Amelia Astor: Enchanted Princess,'" she put air quotes around the words, "brings them out in droves."

"You should have better security," he said, concerned. He continually had to revise his opinion of her. His initial impression of spoiled debutante had been reworked a dozen times already, and he still couldn't figure her out. He wasn't used to being so wrong about people. And God help him, as attracted as he was to her, he was coming to like her. Admire her even.

"I find it works best to play the clueless card. My looks have always helped with that. People assume I'm a certain way because of how I look, or because I'm an Astor. I've been fighting those misconceptions all my life." She shrugged. "But I have a real family on the road and we look out for each other. I don't worry about security. "

"So princesses have groupies?" he said, fascinated and repulsed at the same time.

She seemed to choose her words carefully. "I don't know that I'd call them that. It's not only little girls who come to watch us skate in competition. And in the ice shows sometimes adult men follow us from city to city." She shrugged.

He knew shock must be etched into his face. "When you were a teenager, you had guys—"

"Men."

"*Following* you on the circuit?"

"Fans. Whatever. It wasn't as weird as it is now, after the princess shows."

"Groupies," he said, flatly. "Ever taken anyone up on it?" he asked, his tone even.

"Of course not. I've never been tempted to take money from desperate men. Some of the stuff they've wanted me to do has been pretty benign. I've turned down a handful of proposals— including the marriage kind—and a guy who offered a lot of money for what he called 'foot play.'"

A laugh escaped him.

"Which is totally gross," she continued. "My feet are hideous— calluses, lumps, bumps, and deformities. Skaters have the nastiest feet."

He glanced over. "You know, I remember the moms who came to our shows with their daughters in tow. Invariably one of us, usually Jake or I, would have some cougar, dressed too young and old enough to know better, make an overture. We never, ever followed through on it. We had an unrepeatable name for them and we joked about it, but it was disturbing."

"Wow," she said. "While the moms hit on you, the dads were hitting on me. Maybe they could combine an ice show with a boy band concert and cover all the bases for suburban couple fantasies."

He grinned at her. She was a startling mix of worldliness-- her travel internationally with the ice shows and in competition rivaled his with TruAchord—and naïveté. Despite the differences in their early upbringing, they had quite a bit in common he was startled to realize. If he wasn't careful, they'd end up friends. And he didn't do friendship with women, at least not the kind without benefits, not with someone who looked like her.

Chapter Eight

Shane met her at the rink two days later. For the first time since they'd started training together he was early. He'd been looking forward to seeing her all day. In fact, he found himself wanting to call her, wanting to see her on the days they didn't have practice. It could've been that smokin' hot kiss, it could be he just enjoyed the time together. Whatever it was, it had been six weeks and he was ready. She pulled into the lot in her dinged up Miata and he approached the car, yanking open the door and reaching into the passenger seat where she kept her bag of gear.

Amy smiled. "You're early and you look excited. Did you get the audition?"

"No, they could be weeks or months away from bringing people in," he said, opening the door to the arena for her to precede him. "I'm ready."

She stopped and turned, holding out her arm for the bag. "Ready?"

"Ready to try it with a stick and a puck."

She blinked and pressed her lips together in a gesture he recognized. She was laughing at him.

"Shane. You are nowhere near ready. Your skating is really coming along, I'm so impressed with how much progress you've made," she shook her head, "but adding a stick? That's a level of skill we're not ready for."

"I'm ready," he insisted. How hard could it be? He had the skating down, mostly. He'd brought the pads and gear. He'd even picked up an extra set for her, in what he hoped was her size.

"I can't … we can't, not yet. A few more weeks."

"I know this is your gig, but you'll make the same amount of money whether it takes you six weeks, eight weeks, or sixteen weeks to train me."

The corners of her mouth turned down. Uh oh. That was also an expression he was coming to know.

"Please?" he said, trying to circumvent an argument.

"It's hard for me to coordinate a puck and a stick, Shane, and I've been skating all my life."

"You've played hockey?"

"Just as a goof, against other figure skaters when I was younger. I'm terrible," she admitted. "I don't want you to get hurt and your proficiency isn't there yet."

"I'll gear up."

"You're damn right you will. And," she bit her lip, "I don't care about the money, I don't want you to get injured."

His heart skipped a beat. That's what that expression had indicated. He'd read her wrong, once again. She was hurt, not angry.

She helped him figure out the pads—it was hard to know which way to put on the chest gear, and by the time they were done, they moved stiffly. Amy handed him a helmet, grabbed two pucks and two sticks.

That stick was slightly bigger than she was. Was that a good thing?

"Is your stick supposed to be that long?" he asked.

"Is yours?" she retorted.

He laughed.

"No, it's for someone taller, but I didn't see any shorter ones around here," she shrugged. "No matter."

"Do you know what to do?"

Another shrug, the lips pressed together. "I've seen hockey."

That made him feel better. He'd seen a lot of footage. Studied it. Maybe he'd be teaching her a thing or two.

"What?" she asked, catching what was likely a gleeful expression on his face.

"Nothing. Where are the goals?"

Amy pointed to the far side of the rink. "Two practice goals over there. We should drag them over to this end before we lace up."

By the time they had the goals out on the ice, he could tell Amy was reconsidering the whole thing. The furrow between her sapphire blue eyes was back.

"I really don't know," she said, worrying her full pink lip between perfectly straight white teeth.

Lust surged through him and he looked away, fiddling with the stick, trying to distract himself. "Come on," he wheedled. "It'll be fun. I've got to try it sometime."

He followed her onto the ice, relieved the jersey was like a dress on her. An oversized, polyester dress. He could almost forget what lay beneath.

"We need to warm up. Let's do a few laps with just sticks, get used to the feel, then we'll add the pucks," she suggested.

"We're going to play a little one-on-one though, right?"

She skated backward, shaking her head. "Shane, you are unbelievable."

"That's good, right?"

"Have you always been this competitive?" she asked, giving him and his stick a wide berth as they stroked around the rink.

"I never played team sports, not in any organized way at least. I've played pickup games of basketball here and there."

"I'm surprised. You're an intense competitor. It's obvious just teaching you to skate."

"My parents didn't have the money or inclination to sign me up for soccer or baseball or anything."

"Bummer."

He nodded, and swept past her, eyeing the puck a few feet away. It had sucked. He'd wanted to play a sport for as long as he could remember.

Amy skated up. "There's a league, you know."

"A league?"

"Club hockey, here in LA."

"Even if I had a year of skating with you I won't be good enough for that."

"They have players of all ages and abilities. Women and men. You won't make the A-team, those guys have been on skates from the time they could walk, and scrimmaging and brawling since preschool." She looked over her shoulder and smiled. He nearly lost his footing.

"I didn't know."

Amy skated backward, facing him, the stick barely moving in her arms. "You should look into it. We had one guy—he was a figure skater with Enchanted but he grew up doing both—"

"Do people do both?"

"Sure. He'd play in the summers on the B-team—it goes even lower though, for the real novices. The guy, Mark, he took a lot of ribbing for his day job with us, but he had a great time."

"I'll check it out. Thanks."

Shane went over to adjust the goals, while Amy took a few laps messing with the puck. He watched her struggle with coordinating the puck and stick with her skating.

He looked at her across the center line and recognized the glint in her eye. She may be smiling and relaxed, but she wanted to school him.

His insanely competitive nature gave him no edge at all against her skating. Within ten minutes she's scored two goals and shut him out.

After the second goal she glided up the line, put down her stick and put both hands on her hips.

He scowled inside his helmet.

"If you're not going to play me, I'm not going to do it."

"What are you talking about?"

"I may be faster than you, but you're bigger. You won't come near me! Be aggressive with the puck."

"What do you want me to do? Check you into the boards? I don't want to hurt you, Amy."

"I said I'd play, now play, damn it, and stop treating me like a child, or a *girl*!"

He nodded.

Amy bent down, picked up her stick and held it horizontally between her hands. She came at him, using the stick to push him backward.

"Hey!"

She kept coming, kept pushing with the stick, until he nearly lost his balance. Irritated, he pushed back. The impact was hard enough to send her backward, but instead of landing on her ass, she used the momentum to do a spin and come right back around, laughing at him.

Checking his body hard, she scraped up the puck between them and continued down to score yet again.

Had he really just shoved her back on the ice?

She glided up.

"I'm sorry."

"I'm sorry too," she said, trying to take his stick.

"What are you doing?"

"You can't play me if you're three feet away, so we're done."

"I want to keep going," he insisted, still dumbfounded that he'd pushed her.

"Nope."

"I don't want to get too close, what if I knock up against you or trip you up?"

"What if you do? I'm tough. We could be evenly matched if you would *play*."

He shifted in his skates; he'd worked up a sweat and now that he wasn't moving the moisture was drying, chilling him. She glided toward the barrier, sticks in hand. He left the puck lying on the ice and skated after her.

"Amy, hold up. Maybe I could find someone—"

"I don't know why I'm arguing with you. We should just put this stuff away and go back to crossovers. Or maybe a drill with the sticks." Her expression was irritated. No, more than that, she was mad. Her cheeks bright with temper, lips pressed into a thin line.

Could he do this? It went totally against the grain. But she was right, she had speed and agility on him, the only advantage he had was his size.

"I'm afraid I'll hurt you."

"Don't be a pig."

"I'm not." He put his shoulders back affronted.

Her brows lifted. "You are. You try or we stop, agreed?"

He nodded. Could he even do this?

Thirty minutes later he leaned against the rail. Once he stopped treating her with kid gloves, they were more evenly matched than he would've expected. Sure, she could skate circles around him, and she taunted him with her speed, but her stick handling was atrocious, and when he chased her down, most of the time she choked and missed, and in the battle for the puck, he was able to protect it better than she was.

She came to a stop with the puck in front of him at the line. "You know, figure skaters are way tougher than hockey players. We move at high speed, launch ourselves into the air in a Lycra dress." She tapped her chest. "None of this wussy padding. Trust me. It is way more painful to be a figure skater."

He shook his head. "What about the fights? Getting knocked around?"

"You think I've never ended up in the boards in my leotard? Please. I'm no fragile flower. I've been knocked around for a dozen years."

"Do you have lasting injuries? You said your hip—"

"No," she responded, stepping off the ice. "I'm fine."

"Let's head over to Café Ta for a drink, you up for it?" he asked.

"Sure."

Chapter Nine

Her door flew open and banged into the wall.

Amy jolted upright in bed, staring at the figure of Kyle in her doorway.

"Nailed it!" he sang.

She scrubbed her face and glanced at the clock. 10:00 A.M. "What?" she mumbled.

"Late night?" he taunted.

She glared at him. "Yeah. So?"

"At Café Ta after practice by chance?"

Now how could he possibly know that?

She surged to her knees as the answer hit her.

Kyle nodded. "Yup. You got spotted, babe. And photographed, and speculated about. You're on a few gossip sites this morning." He stepped into her room with his hand up.

Amy squealed and reached up to give him a high-five. "I've got it up on the computer. Get dressed and come see how you look."

Kyle turned on his heel and headed toward the living room.

Amy leaped out of bed to shut the door. *Finally.* She didn't bother to shower, but she brushed her teeth and pulled on her underwear, jeans, and a tank.

Kyle had poured her a cup of coffee by the time she joined him. "Allyson around?"

"She went to visit her parents."

She settled herself on the couch next to him as he pushed the button on his iPad. There they were—Shane was feeding her a bite of something. She sat up straighter in alarm and, judging by his knowing smile, Kyle didn't miss it.

That was the picture they got? Good Lord. Shane was ridiculously photogenic, his expression serious as he leaned over the table toward her. And that picture of her? In a baby doll tee, jeans and sans makeup she looked about eighteen, she thought with a frown.

The camera had only captured her in profile. And that was a blessing. There was something sensual about taking food from his fork, and she'd been so completely caught up in the intimacy of that moment, her stomach had done a barrel roll. . . Kyle waved a hand in front of her face. "Kyle calling Amy. Come in, Amy."

She pushed his hand away, heat rising in her face.

He was grinning, which wasn't her first reaction by a long shot. "What is so amusing?"

"You and him. From fantasy to reality. It's really happening, isn't it? You've lost it over this guy."

"Bullshit." She tossed her hair over her shoulder. "I'm good at faking it."

"You are so not. You have a thing for this one. I've seen this before, babe. It's cool. You know I don't care who you're with only that you don't get hurt. It wasn't fun picking up the pieces after Alexei."

"That was years ago. I'm not that clueless girl anymore."

"Keep it casual. You do casual and this guy Shane," he turned her face to his with a long finger under her chin, "he's bent."

Amy pulled her face away and returned to the picture. Thank God the camera had captured his face instead of hers. She shuddered to think what her expression registered at that moment where her lips wrapped around the steak, before the lust and intensity in his stare. She shivered thinking about it. Thank goodness she hadn't been stupid enough to kiss him again.

She finished her coffee, put the mug down, and bounced on the cushion. "How long till they call?"

Kyle studied the computer screen. "We have four weeks until training starts. My guess is anytime."

"I'm going to shower," she said, grinning. This called for a celebration and she couldn't wait to see Shane.

At 10:35 A.M. Enchanted's general manager, Matt, called her, offering her another year as the lead in the domestic show. She closed her eyes in relief, opened them, and mouthed "stateside" to Kyle, who did a double fist pump. They could've sent her overseas with another crew—not a bad thing, but she'd been in the United States with Kyle the past few years. They were keeping the team together. Amy rolled her eyes as the man on the other end of the line blathered on about the main office and how they'd neglected to send her contract out with the others.

"We'll start training in mid-August, so be ready, the costumes need to fit," the man said. "I'll messenger over the paperwork."

"Of course," Amy replied. "See you at the rink."

Twenty minutes later, Amy came out of the bathroom wrapped in a towel to the sound of a cork popping. She dressed and met Kyle in the kitchen a few minutes later.

"A toast." Kyle handed her a glass of champagne. "To the newest, oldest princess with Enchanted Ice."

Amy stuck out her tongue and clinked his glass. "Cheers."

"Happy now?"

"Ecstatic."

"So how go the lessons?" Kyle asked.

"He's doing really well."

Kyle grinned knowingly.

"No, really he is—he's determined and disciplined. The guy has serious focus," she admitted. "I admire his work ethic."

Amy heard her phone ring in the other room.

Kyle's eyes widened. "Oh my God, Amy, is that … "

Heat seared her neck and washed into her cheeks.

He burst out laughing. "*Drive Me Crazy* is your ringtone for him? And the TruAchord cover of it." Kyle continued to laugh as Amy went into the living room and picked up her phone, breathless.

"You see it?" Shane asked. She could practically hear the smile in his voice.

"See it? I'm *signed*, baby!"

"Fantastic. Let's go celebrate," he said.

"I'm already celebrating," she said, unable to wipe the grin from her face. Her life was back on track, back under her control.

"With Kyle?" he asked, stiffly.

"Yeah. Why don't you come over and have a glass of champagne with us?"

"How 'bout I pick you up in a half hour and we have lunch?"

"That works."

Chapter Ten

Somehow lunch turned into to takeout at his place. She'd only been to his Ocean Avenue condo once before, when she'd dropped him off after the biker plowed into him, and that was only as far as the curb.

He parked the car in the garage and they walked through the tastefully appointed retro style lobby.

"Nice," she said.

"I'm sure it's nothing like what the Astors are accustomed to."

People always assumed that. Her parents had a lot of money. A home in Westchester, an apartment on the Upper West Side of Manhattan. But she hadn't grown up in those places. Home had been a three-bedroom craftsman in upstate New York where she'd lived with her tutor, best friend, and surrogate mother Rowena.

In fact, she'd only been in the New York apartment where her father lived during the week a time or two. Holidays she'd spent in the elaborately decorated house in the affluent New York suburb her mother inhabited, her interactions with her parents as stiff and formal as the furnishings.

It was Shane's level of affluence she was not accustomed to.

His apartment was decorated in a mix of sixties retro style and modern comfort. She glanced around, the décor so perfectly suited to the building, he'd either had a decorator or was hiding some heretofore unforeseen flair. She'd bet the former. She knew set designers and graphic artists with less put together places.

Amy gasped as Shane led her into the living room. The entire wall was curved glass. Through two sets of sliding doors, the Pacific stretched out to the horizon, its surface pricked with whitecaps. Palm trees surrounded a pool that lay below. No rats in these palm trees, they were perfectly manicured.

"Beautiful view," she said, reverently.

"I never get tired of it," he acknowledged, handing her the bag of takeout food. "I'll get some glasses and plates. What do you want to drink?"

"Seltzer?"

He nodded.

Amy opened the door and stepped onto the patio. There was an onshore breeze, but the sun was fierce. She lamented not bringing a hat or a jacket.

Shane came out with the supplies, laid everything down on the patio table and put up the umbrella.

"So thanks again," she said.

"For?"

"For playing the game, for your part in helping me get re-hired."

"You don't have to thank me, I'm sure Ike is ... well, honestly, I'm grateful to you, too. Those photos will do wonders for my bad rep. But I don't want you to think I did it for that reason alone. I am really enjoying hanging out with you. Even if you kick my ass out on the ice."

Amy smiled though her heart skipped a beat at his words. "Am I that bad of an instructor? You push yourself."

"You're a great teacher. And a better hockey player than I ever would have given you credit for."

She hugged herself. The breeze made it chilly in the shade.

"Cold?"

"I'm fine." More nervous than cold, as her teeth were locked together. Her brain couldn't let go of the idea that she was in his house, steps from his bedroom.

He raised a brow and disappeared back inside, returning moments later with a flannel shirt. He held it out and she shrugged into it.

She rubbed her cheek with her shoulder and closed her eyes at the delicious Shane smell emanating from it. She'd assumed it was cologne, but maybe it was some marvelously citrusy laundry detergent mixed with his own scent.

He was studying her curiously.

She froze.

"Would you rather eat inside?" he asked. He laughed at the expression that must have appeared on her face. "Just asking."

"It's amazing," she said, taking in the sight and smell of the ocean only a block from his sixth floor condo.

"It is. And it never gets old. There are a few months where it's foggy and you can't even see the ocean, but then there are times when the ocean is so loud—and the sunsets? I love it," he said simply. "I've been here for six years."

• • •

Shane watched Amy push the lettuce around on her plate. She'd barely eaten anything. "Not hungry?" he asked.

"Oh, no. I am, I'm eating," she replied. "I have to keep an eye on my weight, with training starting. I have costumes to fit into. I tend to gain a little weight when I'm not skating two shows a day. Management will give me no end of grief if they have to alter the costumes."

He eyed her across the table. With all the running she did, he had a hard time believing she'd have difficulty fitting into anything. He'd never been attracted to the ultra thin types—he liked his babes to have some back—and Amy's was damn perfect.

She watched him eat. "It must be nice to not have to worry about it."

He raised his brows and lifted his fork. "I need to gain for the hockey audition, but I've got a few months to add some weight. Want a bite?"

She shook her head and finished her water and smiled shyly at him. He caught his breath. He was used to beautiful people in his line of work. So used to it he hardly noticed anymore that unlike the town of his origins, everyone in this town had perfect hair, teeth, and bodies—money and medical intervention could fix a host of perceived flaws. As the offspring of one of the most privileged families in America, not to mention a world class athlete, Amy had likely been privy to all the benefits of their status from birth: orthodontia, nutritionists, trainers, plastic surgeons, and whatnot. She was stunning, a princess come to life. And it wasn't hair and makeup. He'd seen her sweaty and flushed, both running and skating and even then she radiated a natural unaffected beauty. The hell of it was, over the last few weeks he'd discovered the inside matched the outside.

"So, are your parents psyched you're back in?" he asked.

She laughed. "No. I mean, they don't know and I'm sure if they did know, they wouldn't be pleased. I don't talk to them."

He stopped chewing. "They don't support your career?"

"Hell no. They never recovered from me leaving the circuit."

He put his fork down and sat back in his chair. "Tell me."

"It's a long story." She toyed with her hair and glanced out at the ocean.

"I've got time."

He could see she was debating sharing her personal information with him. The woman was as guarded as they came. "You show me yours, I'll show you mine."

Amy's face relaxed into a smile and his stomach clenched. Hard to believe he'd ever thought she was a soulless beauty queen type. He'd give his left nut to fuck her. But for once he was trying to keep it professional. He enjoyed skating with her, enjoyed being with her, and he didn't want to ruin it the way he usually did.

"My mom had been a gymnast—she was good, college-level good, but she was never great, you know? She had a gymnastics scholarship to Yale and that's where she met my dad. He was— well, he's an Astor."

He nodded. "I can see where this is going."

"Can you? My mother's ambition, my father's money and connections."

"I figured you for a debutante."

"Being a debutante is like … graduation. First there's pre-cotillion, rising cotillion, all sorts of balls and parties and—" she laughed at the look on his face. "I flunked out. Eventually it took too much time away from my training. My mom had me doing dance and gymnastics from the time I was a toddler, but I never took to it. Then one of my mom's friends suggested skating and I loved it." She smiled wistfully.

He pretended to shiver.

"Oh, I know. I loved the cold rinks, the echoes in the building, watching the girls spin in their skirts. I did lessons for a year or two locally, then when I was nine I showed enough aptitude for them to ship me upstate to train with a Russian figure skating coach."

"Nine? Good God. You had to leave your family at nine?"

"Well, it was only my mom. I never saw my dad. He worked eighty-hour weeks, first as an investment banker, then a hedge fund manager.

"That must've sucked."

"You'd think, but it didn't. I had an amazing tutor, Rowena. We lived in a house my parents bought near the rink and did all kinds of fun things—sledding, skiing. Took trips. She was more fun than my parents, and more loving. She gave me a normal childhood. Rowena was the best thing that ever happened to me."

"Is that how you came out of that scene so normal?"

"Ha! I'm not normal. But any bit of normality is thanks to Rowena. She was my best friend, surrogate parent, teacher." *Savior.* "What about you?"

"I was marveling at the similarities in our stories. I was trailer park trash."

She laughed.

"As far as our moms go—my mom was a pageant winner. Mostly small-time stuff. She pushed my sister, Natalie, down that road and I had to go along for the ride. Natalie danced and she was decent, but never did well in competition. Too much pressure and she would choke. I'd have rather played soccer—any sport really, but that wasn't an option. So I learned a little here and there at her lessons. I paid attention, stepped in. There aren't too many boys taking dance lessons in the South, so I was a hot commodity. And it didn't cost my mom anything so she went along. The irony is all of my mother's hopes and aspirations were so wrapped up in Natalie, she didn't notice me—and it turned out, I had reasonable talent."

"Your dad?"

"He's dead," Shane said, briefly.

"I'm so sorry."

He looked away and swallowed hard. "He died when I was twenty-one."

"How sad."

"We weren't close."

"Still."

He changed the subject. "When I was thirteen, my sister got a new voice teacher. She wasn't placing as well in the pageants as my mom would've hoped. I was singing to her, mocking her one day, when we went to pick her up, and the voice teacher, Mrs. James, heard me. She convinced my mother I could sing. I started singing in Mrs. James's church, then soloing at festivals, ballparks. Eventually someone watching a game saw me and thought I had enough talent to audition for a guy who was putting together a boy band. By seventeen I had my GED and was on the road with TruAchord. I don't think my mother ever recovered. She was supposed to live vicariously through my sister's success, not mine.

She attempted to manage my career, but I fired her because she caused ... problems."

"Wow."

He laughed. "Yeah. It was a freight train straight to boy bandom."

"And you're not close with your mom and sister?"

"I'm close with Natalie, but I don't see her much; she's married and lives in Tennessee. My mother? No."

"Gotcha," Amy said softly.

"Can I ask you something?"

"Sure."

He leaned across the table.

"Why do you live in that shitty house in Westwood?"

She broke into a grin that tripled his heart rate.

"Shane, you are the least tactful person I've ever met."

He smiled. He'd heard that before, but coming from her it didn't sound like an accusation.

"Skating for Enchanted isn't lucrative."

He'd thought top skaters made a good income. "That surprises me."

"If you're a former Olympian, you can command terrific money—or at least you could. Some of those ice shows have been on the rocks for years. Some have shut down, others are struggling. Enchanted seems to be doing all right but you'd never know it from what they pay their performers."

"What about your family?"

"I told you, I don't have contact with them, I ran away at seventeen."

"*Ran away?*"

She waved a hand. "It's a long story, and not that interesting."

"Are you kidding? Sounds like a movie of the week."

Amy lips curved, her perfect features radiant. "I've threatened to write a memoir, but my story isn't unique."

"I'd like to know why you quit. You're not a quitter and I've watched your practices, which are incredible."

"Thanks. But the performances we do with Enchanted are nothing like what they do in competition now. With the changes to the programs, there are more jumps required—what I skate in an ice show is about ninety percent less challenging than a competition at an elite level. People often encourage me to get back in, but even if I had the motivation, my body isn't capable of doing those things—not anymore."

"But back then you won practically everything. And you were one of the last women to perform in both pairs and individual competitions. How you could give it all up right before the Olympics?"

Her smile faded and she took a deep breath. "There was a lot of pressure—that's a given. What makes figure skating—and gymnastics and dance—particularly hard is that our bodies change as we mature. Our weight, our height is constantly changing once we hit puberty—you don't want to hear this."

"I do."

She twisted a strand of pale golden hair. "I had done very well in competition the year I turned fourteen. Well enough to get the attention of some of the judges, but later that year, I started having difficulty nailing some of the jumps. A problem I hadn't ever had before. I'd grown, you see—a few inches, put on a couple of pounds. My coach and I were trying to figure out what worked all over again since my shape had changed and my ... er ... development threw off parts of my programs. My parents freaked. They were used to flawless. So they fired my coach, Olga."

"And you liked her?"

"I loved her. Underneath the bluster she had the kindest heart. Olga and Rowena were my family."

"Are you close now?"

"Olga died five years ago—breast cancer."

He watched Amy's eyes fill and took her hand from across the table. She wiped the few tears away that trailed down her cheeks and withdrew her hand to take a swipe at her nose with her napkin.

A knot formed in his stomach as he watched her try to compose herself. What she'd been through with those terrible parents, her coach, on her own at seventeen? How had he misjudged her so thoroughly? His heart ached. Any one of those things: the horrible demanding parents shipping her off at nine, firing the coach she loved, running away, would have destroyed someone else. Yet Amy retained an inner strength and a wide-eyed optimism he envied.

"I'm so sorry." Words were so inadequate. He wanted to wrap her in his arms and protect her.

She shrugged and put the napkin down, picking at her plate. "That was crushing for both of us when she was fired. The new coach. . ." A pained expression crossed her face.

"Tough?"

"Try impossible. She was a terrible fit for me. I was a people-pleaser back then and I wanted to make my parents happy. But Martina Yarotska? I hated her, I feared her. She was a bully and I wasn't tough enough." She cast a look through wet lashes. "I don't think I'll ever be tough enough to go up against someone like her."

His fist clenched in his lap.

"My head was never quite right once I started training with her. From the moment she took over coaching, she pressured me to lose weight. I had to weigh in every morning and if it had risen even a few ounces, she'd post it up on the Jumbotron with … comments."

His fork clattered onto his plate. "What the *fuck*?"

She stared pointedly out at the ocean like it held some kind of secret. "I … I developed an eating disorder," she admitted, haltingly.

He sat back in his chair, stunned. Here was the real reason she'd left competition. "I'm sorry. Did your parents know?"

She shot him a cynical look. "Oh, yeah. Everyone knew. Rowena leaned so hard on my parents to get rid of Coach Yarotska that she nearly got fired. I collapsed a few times."

"*Amy.*"

"At the end the judges were propping me up, giving me high marks for lousy programs. Everyone thought it was temporary—but once I started starving myself, I didn't know how to stop, and my body was not capable of skating when it was deprived that way. The injuries multiplied."

"And so you left—all of it?"

"Yep. Rowena could see what was happening and cared enough about me to intervene. A few weeks after I turned seventeen, I had trouble with my short program. My parents and Yarotska insisted I was only training too hard, but Rowena was worried enough to take me to a doctor. Between them they convinced me that I was killing myself. Once I realized my parents and my coach wouldn't be part of the solution or get me the help I needed, I ran away."

He leaned across the table and took her small hand in his. "I'm so sorry."

"Rowena got me into therapy, I got my GED, and she helped me get my head together. We hid from my parents. I wrote them a letter telling them I was done, but they hired someone to track us down, and they threatened to prosecute Rowena if I didn't go back and re-start my training. I told them if they did that, I'd write my autobiography and it would be worse than *Mommy Dearest.*"

"Amy, I don't know what to say, I'm just so glad you had Rowena. Are you still close?"

Amy pulled her hand away and took a sip of water. "She lives in New England with her husband and three boys. I see her as often as I can. I don't have much family, Rowena and Kyle and the Enchanted skaters, plus the set designers and—" she broke off with a laugh. "I guess I have a big family after all. Once everything went down, my parents left me alone—mostly. I joined Enchanted as soon as I turned eighteen. Rowena wanted me to go to college and quit skating altogether, but I wanted to have fun after being so miserable. I love skating. I promised her I'd go to college eventually." Her face fell. "And I will, but not … yet."

Shane sat back in his chair, practically sitting on his hands to keep from yanking her into his arms and comforting her. Not that she wanted or needed his comfort, but God. Her story, her life, brought out protective instincts in him he didn't even know he possessed. She relayed her story so unsentimentally, but it had to be painful being a commodity. Living someone else's dreams was a burden no one should carry. He should know.

"Did you spend the endorsement money?" he asked.

"What endorsement money?"

"What you got for doing, what was it? Yogurt, car, and … " What was that last one?

"Soup." She narrowed her eyes, the first hint of a teasing spark in her gaze. "Been Googling?"

"Yep."

"I never saw a dime. It all went to my parents."

He moved forward in his chair, staring at her intently. "Some of that money was yours."

"I'm sure it wasn't."

"Amy, you mean to tell me you never saw *any* of it?"

"No, why would I? I was a minor," she said, impatiently.

"Are you for real?"

She scowled and a tiny line appeared between her brows. He itched to smooth it away with his finger. Shaking his head, he said, "Some of that money had to be held in trust for you. Those are big companies you endorsed. Legally speaking, they can't enter into agreements with minors without setting some money aside."

Amy's lips twisted and she cocked her head. "I'm not sure it applies. My parents spent hundreds of thousands of dollars so I could train with the best. It cost upward of fifty thousand a year, plus housing and my tutor."

"That doesn't matter. Your parents can't come after you for training expenses. That's not relevant."

"According to who?"

"I don't know all the ins and outs, but I made money as a minor, too—nothing like what you made since TruAchord didn't really take off until I was over eighteen, but I have a good attorney. Would you be willing to talk to him? Look into it?"

She ran a hand over her mouth. "I don't think that's a good idea."

"Why not?"

"It might bring me into contact with my parents again. I don't want that." Worry marred her perfect features.

"You aren't seventeen anymore. They have no power over you. It might make decisions about life after skating simpler if you have a nest egg. Let him at least look into it for you."

"I can't afford an attorney."

"Don't worry about it."

"No, I really can't. They're hundreds of dollars an hour."

"I'll take care of it, okay? He owes me a favor," Shane lied. "You'll just need to sign something that allows him to investigate. Open and shut. Please?"

Amy sucked her lower lip into her mouth and a surge of lust shot through him.

Quickly, he picked up the plates and carried them through the open sliding door. She followed with their glasses.

God. His hands shook as he walked into the kitchen, rattling the plates. He'd been jonesing for her for weeks. Maybe this time he could have something real, with someone he cared about, without all the restlessness and emptiness that always accompanied his sexual encounters. This time would be different. She was different.

Chapter Eleven

A shiver ran through Amy as she set the glasses on the counter, then put the iced tea back in the fridge.

"Still cold?" he asked, not moving away.

His scent, the heat of his body behind her … every cell in her body was shrieking at her to leave. Bail. Retreat. But Amelia Astor, overconfident and rash as always, pushed Amy's objections aside.

She shook her head and straightened, closing the fridge without turning around. He was so close, she absorbed his warmth through his shirt and her thin dress, heating the skin on her back. She stared at the stainless steel door, hesitant to accept the challenge she knew would be in those cobalt blue eyes. She wanted this. Had wanted this since that first night she'd seen his tall, lean figure in the parking lot of the ice rink. She'd been desperate for it since that night at Spoke.

She could handle a physical relationship. Now that she had a job starting in a few weeks, whatever she and Shane started had an automatic expiration date. All her relationships did. There was something liberating about knowing the end was near at the onset.

He stroked his fingers down her arms, lightly. But instead of tickling, it started a throb, and she trembled. His hot, hard palm replaced his fingers as he smoothed them over her body, tugging his shirt off her shoulders, exposing and shaping her curves under the dress. Skimming lightly at first, then with firm pressure over her breasts, he ran them down to the indentation of her waist, then smoothed his hands over her ass.

She heard the hiss of his indrawn breath.

His hands went down the hem of her baby doll dress and lifted, sliding those scalding fingers into the curve of her buttocks, shaping them roughly, dragging up the material.

"God, Amy. Your body is amazing."

She closed her eyes. His breath was humid against her neck. He used a hand to move her heavy blonde mane aside and pressed his lips to the erratic pulse there.

Shane fitted his hands under the dress, and using his arms to hitch it up, he moved his palm around, across her taut stomach, slowly upward exploring her flesh, finding the mound of first one breast then the other.

"Take a breath," he muttered.

She gasped.

His touch seared through the thin lace of her demi-cup bra. Long fingers released the front clasp, and Amy pressed her palms against the steel of the fridge as he pushed the material aside to roll her nipple between his thumb and forefinger.

She bit her lip to keep from moaning, then glanced down to see his wide palm cupping the weight of her breast under the dress, fingers stroking, gently scissoring the pebbled tip until she cried out.

His tongue traced the overheated flesh of her neck, and she tilted her head to give him better access while his other hand dipped down, back over her abdomen—stroking down her thigh. Her head swam; her body too lethargic and overwhelmed to do more than feel, she leaned more of her weight into her arm, pressing against the cold stainless steel appliance in front of her.

She widened her stance, desperate to have him inside. Her body was an insistent, painful ache.

She pushed back with her hips and rocked them against the front of his jeans. He groaned, cupped her sex in one hand and used it to stroke her backside against his erection. A finger slid into the front of her panties to tease her, and he growled his satisfaction at finding her slick heat. One finger pressed inside; she ground down on his palm and her legs shook so badly, she laid her cheek to the fridge and gripped the door handle.

The hand playing with her nipples became more aggressive, pinching and pulling, startling, while his other hand stroked her sex softly—too softly.

Amy bucked into his hand, her breath coming in pants. She tried to turn around, but he stayed her, holding her overheated body to the unyielding surface of the refrigerator.

"No, like this," he muttered.

He pushed another finger into her, and her legs spread wider of their own volition. He pumped his fingers into her, then removed his hand at her drawn-out moan.

Grabbing her wrist, he towed her down the hall, into a bedroom at the end. She was only vaguely aware the room had the same view of the ocean as he led her to the bed, directing her onto her knees on the edge, facing away from him. Lifting the dress over her head, he tossed it. He peeled off her bra, then her panties. Gently he applied pressure to the center of her back until she was on all fours, shivering, her breath coming in gasps.

She tried to turn but again he stopped her. She heard the rustle as he removed his own clothes, the draft of air that hit her overheated body as he whipped off his shirt, the rasp of the zipper before he shucked his jeans and boxer briefs.

Through the curtain of her hair she turned to watch as he covered his straining erection with a condom. Where had that come from? She wanted to face him—the pressure of his hand in the center of her back stayed her.

He murmured her name and used his hands to spread her thighs wider. The ache in her sex was intolerable.

She turned her head and met his eyes. "Shane, hurry up."

He worked the thick head of his cock against her, readying her, but she was there—slick and desperate, Amy pushed back against him.

With a grunt he worked the wide tip into her; she was beyond aroused, but it had been a few months and her flesh stung as he pressed forward. Discomfort blended with desperation. Amy twisted her hips, trying to accommodate his girth.

"God, you're so fucking tight," he ground out.

He withdrew and worked his way halfway in again, grasping her hips and spreading her, holding the juncture where her thighs met her buttocks. He thrust all the way in and she gasped with the mingled pleasure-pain.

He reached around to rub her with his hand. She rocked against him, her body trying to accommodate his length, each rough thrust sending her reeling toward completion. Desperate, she barely registered the gasping, sobbing noises emanating from her throat.

She found his balls, already high and tight against his body.

"Aww fuck, Amy," he gasped out and his hand moved on her with lightning speed as he doubled his pace. She dropped her head into the sheets as she rocketed into her orgasm, crying out his name.

He pounded into her hard and fast, long and deep. She pushed her fingers up into the space behind his balls, stroking him there until, with two more thrusts so rough he drove her body up onto the bed, he came with a shout.

He collapsed next to her on the mattress, his body heaving, grinning.

"That was awesome."

She smiled, moved to her side and propped her head on her hand. "It was."

She couldn't worry about how this would affect their burgeoning friendship, or their lessons. She would take Kyle's advice. Casual. Besides, Enchanted and the road were only weeks away. She did have a no-sex-with-co-workers mandate, but that had been established because she'd caught her first love—the lead prince and a man ten years her senior—cheating on her. Giving Shane skating lessons was hardly the same thing.

There had been serious relationships since then, but infrequent flings on the road were the norm. These days anything that could be termed a relationship happened during summer when Enchanted was on hiatus. And no matter how intense it started, there was a September expiration date. Shane was no different.

Chapter Twelve

"Fuck," Shane said. Why did good things always go to hell when women were involved? Apparently the fact that he and Amy had spent the last two weeks between his sheets learning every inch of each other's bodies didn't always translate into a satisfying ending.

He rolled off Amy onto the bed and covered his face with his arm, hiding behind his elbow.

"What the fuck?" he said again.

"It happens."

He lifted his arm, turned his head, and glared at her. "Not to me it doesn't."

She sat up. "Great. Thanks." She stood, scooped up her scattered clothes, moved into the bathroom, and slammed the door.

Goddamn it. Now she was pissed at *him*, when this whole thing was her fault. Sure it had happened—a handful of times—usually when he'd made the mistake of mixing sex with an abundance of alcohol in his youth. Shit. How could he have lost his erection? He'd been rock hard and desperate for her.

If only she hadn't insisted on turning over. He didn't *do* missionary. He'd be happy with her on top and from behind was always amazing. But why did she have to insist on *that*? All that heavy eye contact. The position was altogether too personal.

He pulled on his jeans and went to the bathroom door. "Amy? I'm sorry. I was," he searched for the word that would pacify her, "insensitive. Can you … come out here?"

There was silence behind the door.

"Amy?"

The door opened and she stood there fully dressed, avoiding his eyes. "I'm going home," she said softly.

Shane ran a hand through his hair. "Amy. I … that doesn't happen. And I don't know why it did. Why don't we get something to eat and try again later?"

"No thanks. I got mine and I have plans."

"Since when?" What the hell was wrong with her?

She met his eyes and he registered what was on her face—it wasn't anger, or disappointment, or disgust. It was hurt. And it made his chest ache.

"Look, it's no big deal—" he tried.

"It is to me."

"Really?" *What the hell?* "We've had amazing sex a dozen times and this one time—"

"And why couldn't you? Do you even know?" she asked.

He was instantly on the defensive. "There's no reason for it. This shit happens. Every once in a while you can't get there. It's never happened to you?"

"Of course I've had sex without being able to come. And of course some positions work better than others, but you can't have sex with me missionary style, can you?"

He backed up a step.

"That's not—"

"That *is* why. You're always trying to flip me onto all fours or make me ride you. *Always.*"

"So?" He looked up at the ceiling. "I like watching you, Amy." Every guy had his preferred positions. There was nothing weird about that.

"You can watch me in any position."

He shifted awkwardly. "You're making a big deal about nothing. It's just sex," he blurted.

Her body froze and her eyes widened a fraction. She put a hand on his chest and gave him a shove, hard.

Four long strides took her out of the bedroom.

He followed, naked.

She grabbed her purse from the table near the front door.

He followed her. "Amy, what's going on?"

"You're right," she said, her voice quiet and cold. "It's just sex. Bye, Shane. See you at the rink."

She slammed the door behind her.

He stood staring, open-mouthed. What the fuck just happened? Had she ended things? Because he had ... difficulty? Once? That was ridiculous. They'd had sex, sometimes more than once a day, and that was it? He hadn't been tempted to hook up with anyone else for the first time since he could remember. He liked her.

Was she going back to Kyle? That guy wanted her. She could deny they had something, but he'd seen the way Kyle looked at her. The way all men looked at her. Like they wanted to defile her fifty different ways. And he'd be Goddamned if he'd let her go like that.

He nearly tripped in his haste to dress, grab his keys, and slam the front door before he realized it was too late to catch her. He didn't know where she'd gone and they didn't have practice tonight.

He'd made dinner reservations at that little Italian place in Malibu.

He let himself back into his apartment and called her.

No answer. Called again. She still didn't pick up.

He texted her. "I'm sorry. Please come back."

He waited ten minutes. There was no response.

"Give our," his fingers paused over the key pad as he slowly typed out the twelve-letter word that left him lightheaded and nauseated, "relationship a chance, please. I'm so sorry." But it was a relationship. With someone he liked and admired. He had to step up his game with her. She would accept nothing less.

Fifteen minutes later there was a knock at his door. He flung it open. Amy stood in the hallway, eyes red-rimmed, and her skin blotchy. He yanked her into his embrace with trembling arms.

• • •

Until the fight, Amy had split her time between him and her skating friends, staying over at her own place alone nearly as many as she'd stayed in his bed. But since that night, he was jealous of her time. He'd insisted on her staying. They'd stopped to get some of her things and she'd been quasi-living with him from that point.

Rather than the normal feelings of panic he experienced when someone stayed over, he stressed about the clock ticking on their time together. She'd already explained that she didn't do the long distance thing. Ever.

Their days started to fall into a familiar pattern: running every morning on the days he didn't meet his trainer, followed by fooling around in the kitchen, shower, balcony—oh, the sex they'd had out there. He shook his head, grinning. Good thing he wasn't A-list or there'd be video circulating about now.

They lazed away the rest of the day until skating practice—some days he read scripts and she read books. She could sit on his patio and curl up with a book for hours on end—and she was fast, too. She'd even started to read through some of his pile of scripts, insisting he couldn't put all his eggs in the hockey movie basket.

She'd had been excited about one script in particular, a comedy where they were looking to cast him as a dimwitted army captain. She had giggled her way through when she read it to herself, then insisted he run through some lines with her. Amy laughed uproariously at his deadpan delivery. She'd sworn it was made for him and so he tossed it into his new "to be considered" pile.

Then an hour into practice on Tuesday night, his phone rang while they took a water break. His agent. Shane's heart, already racing from the crossovers she'd had him doing, accelerated still further.

"Yeah?"

"Your mother's in the hospital," Ike said.

"So?"

"So, why the fuck aren't you there?"

" 'Cause I'm here learning to skate—not that I'd go anyway, my mother is a—"

"I don't care if your mother is a three-toed sloth, Shane. Image, son, image. You have a choice of two roles you play in this situation: concerned son or asshole."

He sighed. "How do you even know this?"

"How do I know anything?" Ike said. "It comes over the wires. I have alerts set for all my clients. She's been on the news in Podunkville, Tennessee."

Shane rubbed his brow. "It'll blow over."

"Get your ass to Podunkville. Pronto."

"But the skating—"

"Take her with you, they have rinks there." The other man hung up.

The last fucking place he wanted to go. The last fucking person he wanted to see. Take Amy? No way. There weren't any skating rinks within a hundred-mile radius of his hometown. Likely Memphis or Nashville though. And then it would be all over the news if he showed up to skate there. No thanks.

Amy had skated off to give him privacy, but as he walked over toward the ice, she glided up. "What's up?" she asked, taking in the expression on his face.

"Apparently I need to get my ass home." Every instinct he had was shrieking at him to leave it at that, but not even his fears of her exposure to his mother could over-ride his desire to have her with him. "Ever been to the Volunteer State?"

She grinned. "I've been everywhere with Enchanted, Shane. Yes, I've been to Tennessee, and it was hotter than hell when I was there in October. You want me to come with you in August?"

"Yes."

Chapter Thirteen

His phone rang and he glanced at the number. "Amy, do you mind getting that? It's my sister," Shane said as he steered the rental car down the two-lane highway toward his hometown of Tyler, Tennessee.

"Hi, Natalie. It's Amy, Shane's friend."

Shane frowned. She needed to quit with that friend bullshit and call him her boyfriend.

"Oh, really? Okay. We're on Route 40 at … " She glanced at Shane with raised eyebrows.

"An hour away."

She told Natalie where they were and then pressed the phone to her chest. "Your mom's been discharged. Your sister's got her settled in. Now Natalie's at her own house and wants to know if you could stop by on your way to your mom's."

"Tell her of course."

"Shane says of course," she relayed. "Okay. See you soon."

"She's already been discharged?" Amy asked, though whether surprised or impressed he couldn't tell. He nodded. "I'm sure she insisted on it. It's too soon, but she probably wanted to get home to start smoking again."

Amy's eyes widened. "Wow."

"Yeah."

She looked out the window. "Shane, it is so gorgeous here. I can't get over how green it is—and these rolling hills."

"Mmm hmm," he muttered, distractedly.

"What?"

"Wondering what's going on with Natalie."

"You guys are close, right?"

He shrugged. "We were. Growing up, it was the two of us against the world, or at least against my mom. Nat and her husband, Jesse, live nearby. My mom is … well, you'll see. She's a tough nut."

"Well, she'd have to be if she left the hospital after a heart attack so she could go home and smoke," she replied.

His lips twisted. "I'm serious, Amy, she's not a nice person. Be on your guard with her, okay? If you don't let her in, she can't hurt you."

She shot him a curious look.

Forty minutes later they turned off the highway onto a two-lane road, then onto a gravel driveway. A modest ranch house sat nestled under a few giant oaks.

Amy stepped out of the car and her stretch lifted the baby doll t-shirt to bare her flat stomach. He'd had her at zero dark thirty this morning and considered stopping at some fleabag motel to have her again. Instead of falling into any kind of sexual normalcy, his desperation for her grew exponentially. He adjusted his jeans as his erection swelled.

Amy caught the motion and the expression on his face and grinned. "You're insatiable, Shane Marx." He reached her in five strides as she backed away laughing. He took her by the shoulders and pressed her body up against the hood of the car. Dipping his head, he found her laughing mouth. She turned her head away. "Shane! Anyone in there can see us."

"So what?" He set her on the hood of the car, and stepped between her legs. Widening his stance, yanking her knees on either side of his hips, he took her lush mouth, stroked his tongue into her moist, minty cavern, and swallowed her moan.

He was desperate to fuck her, to get out of his own head. He lifted her skirt; his hand rubbed over her silky thigh and made straight for her panties.

Amy leaned her head back. "Shane?"

He recaptured her mouth, sliding the palm of his hand to cup her mound. He could feel her, hot and damp through the cotton. His hand moved to the front of his jeans.

"Shane!" She put both her hands on his chest and shoved.

He took two startled steps back. "What?" he ground out.

"What's the matter with you? We're in the driveway of your sister's house," she snapped, hopping off the hood. "Get a grip, would you?"

He raked a hand through his hair.

Amy grabbed her purse off the ground and held it in front of her, wide-eyed and irritated.

"Sorry," he muttered, leading the way up down the walkway to his sister's front door. Behind him Amy muttered about grown men who behaved like teenage boys and making good impressions.

What had he been thinking? He hadn't, that much was obvious. He hated being back here.

His sister opened the door before he knocked and from the grin on her face she'd seen them going at it by the car.

Natalie held him tightly. Her body was a shade rounder and her narrow face wreathed in smiles. "God, Shane. It's been too long!"

"I know, Nat. I wish you would come out to California and see me more often. Hey, this is Amy Astor," he narrowed his eyes at her, "my girlfriend."

Amy smiled and shook hands with Natalie, who pulled her into an embrace instead.

"Girlfriend?" his sister thunked him on the back, "and one you bring home for a change? Will wonders never cease? Come on in and sit down. I made coffee 'cause I figure you all have been traveling since the butt-crack of dawn."

When they had settled onto the couch in the sunroom, Natalie perched on the edge of her seat across from them, lacing and unlacing her hands as she attempted small talk.

Shane couldn't take it anymore. "Out with it. Is it Mom?" he interrupted.

"Is what Mom?"

Shane took a sip of his coffee. "Whatever has you so keyed up, Nat."

"Oh. That. No. Mom's the same." She looked Amy up and down. "Avoid being alone with her," she suggested.

Amy cocked her head. "Excuse me?"

"She's a nasty piece of work." Natalie eyed Shane before continuing, "Frankly, I'm astonished you came back after all she's done." But there was no judgment in her tone.

"Same goes. Why are you helping her?"

"Someone had to drive her ass from the hospital home—I wore earplugs and cranked the radio."

Amy's eyes darted to his.

"She'll be fine, you know. She's a tough, mean old bird," Natalie said.

"So why are you so on edge?"

Nat glanced over at Amy.

Amy caught the look and stood. "I'll go refill my coffee, if that's okay."

She waved her down. "No worries, hon, it's not top secret." But his sister twisted her hands together in her lap. "Jesse and I have been trying to have a baby."

"Okaaay," he said.

"For the last five years."

Shane stiffened. "What's wrong?"

"We don't know exactly, but I've never been able to conceive. We've, uh. . ." She took a deep breath.

Amy pulled her hair back and gestured to the other room. "I don't want to make you uncomfortable. Why don't I ... "

Shane's sister shook her head. "No, it's okay. We've done a few procedures, small stuff—but nothing's covered by insurance."

Shane relaxed back into the couch. "Nat, you know I'm happy to do whatever you need."

"Well, we've exhausted our savings—between Jesse's contracting business slowing down with this economy and my income, well, we can't swing anymore and … "

"Whatever you need," he repeated. "Money? Or do you want to come to California to try? We must have good clinics for that."

"No, no. We've been happy with our doctor. It's that, well, if we do the in-vitro thing, it's really expensive. We're also considering adoption, which is nearly as much. Our real concern is that we'll spend so much money trying to have a child that by the time we get one, we won't be able to provide for it."

Shane studied his sister, but Natalie's light-blue gaze wouldn't meet his. "What's this about, Nat? You know I'd give you anything."

She sighed. "Jesse."

Shane sat back, blowing out a breath.

Natalie rubbed a hand across her eyes. "I've decided to borrow from you and not tell him. I'm going to use the frozen stuff we have and … do the procedure. If it works, he'll be happy." Tears filled Natalie's eyes and she caught her breath on a sob. "There's no other way. I want a baby so badly and he won't … he won't."

Shane went over and knelt in front of his sister, taking her hands. "Natalie. Don't do that."

She wrenched her hands away. "You don't know what it's been like. For years, Shane. For years we've tried and tried, and hoped and prayed. I've taken hundreds of those damn ovulation predictor tests and pregnancy tests if I'm even a half day late. Nothing," she said dully. "Now we're here, at the end of the line financially. We got a second mortgage on the house. We tried three times the less invasive way. It didn't work. Nothing has worked," she repeated, brokenly.

"I'm so sorry, Nat. I'll write you a blank check. But if you don't get Jesse's consent, he won't forgive you."

"He will," she insisted. "He'll forgive me when he's holding our baby in his arms. He'll let go of his damned pride then."

"Let me talk to him."

His sister shook her head. "You know he won't listen to you." She bit her lip and grabbed for his hands, but Shane had already stood.

"He'll never let that go, will he?"

Natalie put her head in her shaking hands.

Amy scooted up to him and took his hand.

His body vibrated with guilt and anger.

Natalie glanced at Amy. "She doesn't—"

"No," he bit out. "Does he even know I'm in his house?" he asked.

"No," his sister said softly.

"God, Nat. I'm sorry. But I can't be responsible for another rift. The first one is bad enough. Get him on board—"

"Don't you think I've tried?" she wailed.

He stood, pulling Amy to her feet.

"I'm sorry. Fuck, am I ever sorry, Sis. If I could go back and fix it, I would. But I won't give you money that ends your marriage."

He strode out the front door, leaving his sister sobbing on the couch. Amy trailed after him. He unlocked her car door and held it for her. Shutting it and going over to his side, he put the key in the ignition and backed up so fast, gravel spat from under the tires.

They drove for ten minutes in silence. Before they got to the highway, Shane turned onto another gravel road with a curse. He put the car in park and pounded on the steering wheel.

"Fuck, fuck, *fuck*!"

Amy sat silently.

He grabbed her by the back of the head and pulled her over into his lap, kissing her desperately. She crawled over and straddled him, pushing the seat back as far as it would go. He licked into her mouth, holding her hips down on his erection. Amy tried to soothe him, stroking his back and murmuring, but he wanted none of that. No tenderness. He had to have her. Now.

He peeled her panties down from under her dress; in her contortions to get them off, her knee jabbed into him and he didn't care.

He cursed, hands moving to his fly while he lifted his hips and struggled with his jeans.

"Wait, Shane, wait," she mumbled into his mouth. "Do you have something?"

His hands stilled and he swore. "In the trunk."

She moved off until she was lying half on the gearbox, head in his lap.

Was she. . . "No Amy," he tried to pull her up, "you don't have to do that."

"I know I don't have to," she said, wetting her lips she glanced from him to his cock. He groaned, thickening with anticipation. "I want to." She worked him free of the bunched jeans. She tilted her head, watching him.

He couldn't take his eyes off her glistening lips, her pink tongue peeking out.

He groaned and slid down in the seat as she gave him a few experimental strokes.

"Amy," he panted. "Amy."

She teased him at first. And when he was well beyond teasing, she sucked strongly until her cheeks hollowed, then licked the underside decisively. How could he be on the verge so soon? She'd just started.

"Amy ... I'm close," he said hoarsely, but the sight of her working his cock, looking up at him sent him right to the edge.

"Mmmm," she mumbled, her mouth full, her hand pumping the base of his shaft.

"Amy," he gasped. "Please … fuck … stop. If you don't want … I can't … " And then it was too late, she was taking all of him.

Afterward he sat in the seat, calm and relaxed for the first time in hours, staring down at her. Feeling like this after sex was a revelation. There was no shame. No panic. None of the usual anxiety about how to extricate himself from the person he was with. He helped her across to his side of the car and cuddled her against his chest. Here was this woman he'd thought was spoiled. Instead she turned out to be generous, sympathetic, and hotter than hell. He hadn't anticipated finding someone he cared about this much about. Their first few weeks in Los Angeles had been so blissful, he hadn't even noticed other women. Hadn't cared. But lately he'd more than noticed. The more he tried to push away the fantasies, the harder they were to stifle. Thoughts about the checkout woman at the grocery store—hell, he'd gotten worked up fantasizing about the flight attendant in first class on the way here while Amy slept in the window seat next to him. Guilt rolled through him.

Apparently being with one person, faithful and happy, wasn't part of his repertoire. If he cared about her as much as he did, why were the temptations coming back?

He reached into the cooler in the backseat, handed a bottle of water to her and she drank, gratefully.

His body still trembling, he took out another water and finished it, crushing the plastic and tossing it into the back seat. She made a move to slide back over to her side of the car, but he held her tightly, his heart still racing. "Thank you."

"You don't have to thank me," she whispered with a shake of her head, grinning. "It's not like you haven't done that for me, countless times."

"I know, but here. And like this." He gestured to the car.

She shrugged. "Figure skaters are flexible. And adaptable. You needed it."

He crushed her up against him and admitted what he could no longer keep inside. "I'm crazy about you, Amy Astor, and it scares the holy hell out of me."

• • •

Amy watched Shane steer the car back onto the highway.

"You wanna tell me about it?" she asked.

"No."

"Shane."

She resettled back in her seat waiting, fearful. Her gut clenched.

"I fucked my brother-in-law's sister."

"Oh." That was not good, and guys could be weird about their sisters' sex lives—at least from what she'd gleaned from Kyle's relationship with his. But surely if they were both consenting adults? Her body relaxed.

It bubbled out of him. "It was at Nat's wedding. And Danica was married. She has a big mouth—everyone knew by the end of the weekend. Her husband divorced her and she's been married twice since then—she's not even thirty. So Jesse hates my guts. And he'll never let Natalie take anything from me—hell, I can barely see her without causing problems between them. If I give her money, it will end them. For her sake, I try to stay away." He rubbed his mouth. "I love my sister, but I made a mess of things. Jesse's not a bad guy, but he's an angry, stubborn son of a bitch."

"God." She felt his eyes on her and tried school her features into something other than disgust. He was going too fast to keep looking over at her the way he was—probably trying to gauge her reaction. She met his glance with an attempt at a reassuring smile that must've had the opposite effect.

"I know," he said. "It's a screwed up situation. I've tried talking to Danica, to Jesse—it's useless."

"Try again," she suggested. "You're both older—you've changed." But had he? She hated to keep thinking about his past, since most of what she knew was gossip and rumors, he was tight-lipped about his history. She'd known he had issues with this stuff from the onset. There was something about the way he looked at women that made her uncomfortable. It wasn't anything as blatant as flirtation, nothing like he'd been with that waitress at Spoke, but he exhibited a level of awareness—like with the flight attendant on the way here—that tied her stomach in knots. If it had been less subtle she would've said something.

"And say what?" he said.

"That you're sorry? That you were stupid?"

"Do you think I haven't tried that over the years? And all the shit that continues to come down about my life adds fuel to his fire."

Silence reigned in the car for several miles. At least he was able to associate his problems with his past with the problems in his present. That was good, right?

Chapter Fourteen

The next day Amy popped her head in Mandy Marx's open door. "I'm heading downstairs, can I get you anything?"

"I could use some company," Mandy said in her thick Tennessee drawl that made Amy smile. The woman indicated the overstuffed recliner in the corner of the massive suite, a few feet away.

The poor woman, alone in this enormous house. A house that TruAchord's money had built, no doubt. Her husband was dead and her kids wanted nothing to do with her. And yet she'd been so gracious in her vulnerability. She was a tiny little thing, barely five-foot-three, and all the coffee and cigarettes kept her lean. But she looked older than her years, and according to Shane, she had a lot of vices.

"Of course."

Mandy's smile was sweet and Amy relaxed into the chair. Granted they'd only been here a day, but there was nothing about this woman to indicate she was as difficult as Nat and Shane said. Mandy Marx wasn't a monster.

"So, darling, how did you meet my Shane?"

"We both live in LA and he's ... " She hesitated. Surely it wasn't a secret from his mother? "He's been learning to skate for an upcoming role, so I've been working with him."

"Right. You're the skater who quit all those years ago. You couldn't handle the bigger contests?"

Amy stiffened. "No, actually. I ... it wasn't a healthy environment for me."

Mandy Marx narrowed her eyes, but her face was set in compassionate lines. "Poor dear. You need a will of iron and self-disciple to succeed at the top levels. Don't I know it. My Natalie didn't have it either."

Amy swallowed and tried again. "It wasn't anything to do with my will—"

"No? 'Cause looking at you, angel, I'm thinking maybe it was the self-discipline part. For a skater, you're … a big girl. Was that always the problem? That was a problem with my own daughter. She couldn't keep the weight off to be world-class. Some women don't have what it takes to be their best selves."

Amy sat back in the chair, heart slamming around in her chest. The heat rose in her face. Had this woman just called her *fat*?

"You know," Shane's mother continued, conversationally, "don't take it to heart that Shane looks at other women—he always has. Those girls who were over yesterday?"

Amy pressed her lips together. The twenty-year-old twins who had used Mandy's health as an excuse to bring food and flirt with Shane? He had been distantly polite, but, ever vigilant, she'd caught his covert, heated glances at them during their brief visit. It made her ill. Apparently he was looking for something—for someone else.

"He's always liked Southern women. Well, there's not lot he doesn't like as you probably know." She laughed delightedly and Amy recoiled, her skin like ice.

"A lot of men don't tell you what does it for them, and they'll make do for a while, but I happen to know Shane likes his women tiny. You can never be too rich or too thin, but as long as you have one of those two things going for you, Amelia. . ."

Now Amy noticed what she hadn't before. The cold, calculating depths of those pretty, wide, aquamarine eyes.

She stood without another word and strode out of the room, reeling from the attack. She made her way to the landing, holding her churning stomach, and scurried down the stairs. Shane looked up from the bottom of the steps, one foot on the riser.

"Amy?"

She brushed by him with a muttered "later" on her way to the front porch. The air was thick with humidity and the smell of vegetation—and it was barely 10:00 A.M. She had to get out of there.

The street was quiet—perhaps a walk or run would release some of her pent up rage and humiliation. Before she could commit, however, the screen door slammed and Shane's arm came around her shoulders. She shrugged it off, wrapped her arms around herself, and took two steps down the porch into the sun.

"Did you tell her?"

"Tell her what?"

"About my struggles with food." She faced him to gauge his reaction, her vision blurred by tears.

His mouth dropped. "Fuck no."

His body went rigid as he turned back to stare at the house. Without a word he went back inside.

She heard raised voices. Shane's furious cursing, his mother's plaintive tones. Moments later he returned with his keys and her purse. He handed it to her and took her other hand.

"C'mon."

They drove back to the two-lane divided road in silence. Halfway to the hotel, Shane pulled off onto the shoulder. "There. See that tree?" He pointed to a large oak in the forest on the side of the road. She glanced over at his expressionless face, sunglasses hiding his eyes. She nodded slowly and he pulled back onto the road.

"That's where my dad killed himself."

"*Shane*. I thought he died in a car accident."

"Yep."

"But ... "

"Do you know how many single car accidents are suicide? I'm sure it was in his case. He was healthy. The autopsy showed he died of traumatic injuries from the wreck, not a heart attack or seizure or something."

"Maybe he lost control or nodded off—"

"No. He killed himself to get away from her."

Amy stared at him in horror. If his mother had done that kind of damage to her spouse, what had she done to Shane and his sister? She shifted uneasily in the seat. "You can't know that."

"Can't I?" He turned into the parking lot of the motel, shut off the engine, and opened the driver's side door. She was still sitting stunned in the passenger seat when Shane came around to open the door and help her out. She followed him into his hotel room.

He tossed his sunglasses, keys, and wallet onto the desk and sat on the bed, pulling her down beside him. She sat cross-legged, facing him on the threadbare orange and brown comforter.

Shane stroked the fingers of one hand down her face. "Whatever she said—"

"She said I was too fat to be a figure skater."

He inhaled sharply. "That bitch."

"Or to be with you. In the guise of being helpful."

"When she's not being passive aggressive, she's outright aggressive. I'm so sorry, Amy. She's cruel and manipulative and a bully. We shouldn't have come."

He would get no argument from her. And he hadn't contradicted what his mother had said about her being fat. Maybe she was putting on a few pounds. Maybe that's why Shane was still eyeing other women. It astonished her how much it hurt to see him give those twins—and the flight attendant—the once over.

That's why this needed to come to an end. As soon as her plane took off, this relationship was over. It was only a few weeks until she went on the road for eight months. Couldn't he wait that long? Or maybe he was the type of guy who had to line up the next thing before the first thing was over. She shuddered, wrapping an arm around her abdomen. The end couldn't come soon enough, because she had fallen for Shane, hard. He was still tactless, but she now found his directness refreshing. He was considerate and caring. Maybe that was the Southerner in him. She pushed those thoughts away. "And your dad?"

"Dad was … not a strong person. He wasn't capable of defending my sister and I. He appreciated having kids because it deflected some of her venom," he said, bitterly.

She reached for his hand and threaded her fingers through his.

"With us both out of the house, her viciousness turned on him, it was more than he could take. And he had his own issues with depression and avoidance. She's a pariah." Shane shrugged.

"I guess that explains your … "

He frowned. "What?"

Amy's mouth twisted. This was the wrong time to bring this up. The absolute worst time. She was still shaky from his mother's nastiness and his revelation about his father. She would not bring up the other part of what his mother had said. "Never mind, Shane."

He drew back. "No. I want to know what you were going to say."

She shook her head and tried to take his hand back, but he stood.

"Tell me."

Amy rubbed a hand across her mouth. Her stomach twisted into a knot. "Your attitude toward women."

He stiffened. "What attitude?"

She shrugged. "It's that after meeting your mother and knowing what life must've been like in TruAchord, I can see where women are. . ."

"Are what?"

"Your experiences haven't been good," she hedged.

Tension hummed between them.

"Shane, I don't want to fight."

He scowled. "Amy, you can't say something like that after meeting my mom and hearing about my dad. I want to know what the hell you're talking about."

Amy rubbed her face with both hands. It wasn't the confrontation that sickened her—but there wasn't any tactful way to say it.

"You don't have a good history with women. I only meant I could see why."

Anger emanated from him in waves, his lips clamped together.

"Please, Shane, let's not do this now, here."

"I love women, too much maybe," he said.

She stared at him, aghast. "No, you don't."

"I have a past, Amy, and there are a lot of women in it. If that bothers you. . ." He shrugged.

"I understand your past, Shane. But those weren't all relationships, were they? And it's not only that. It's the way you look at women, even when we're together. And what you've said about them."

"I don't know what you're talking about." He towered over her, arms folded across his chest, blocking her ability to stand.

She pulled her knees to her chest and hugged them to her.

"You size women up. Everywhere we go. And yeah, it's disturbing, now that we're ... together."

"So what if I notice attractive women? I'm not stepping out on you."

"Aren't you?"

"What the fuck, Amy? I've been faithful."

"Have you really, I mean, in your head?"

"What?" he said, harshly.

"It's not that you notice women." She paused, trying to put into words what bothered her most about his mother's comments. "It's the way you look at them, like you're fantasizing about bending them over the nearest object."

He backed away from her, the skin over his cheekbones flushed with anger, his hands clenched into fists. He laughed, but it was forced. "So now you know what I'm thinking? I had no idea you were so insecure."

"Fuck you. Men who do what you do—ogle women—always say 'don't be insecure, baby, if I appreciate what's out there. I'm not going to stray' or 'all men do it, whether you notice or not.' But I *am* secure in myself. The way you look at other women when we are out doesn't say anything about me, but it says a whole helluva lot about *you*." Now if she could convince herself of that, she'd be golden.

He stared at her clenched jaw. "What does it say?"

"That you're a man who objectifies women. You did it to me, too, before you knew me. Before we became friends. But it's more understandable now. I mean, if I were raised by Mandy Marx, I'd be a misogynist too."

"A w*hat?*"

"A misogynist. It's a—"

"I know what the word means, Amy. I don't know how you could apply it to *me*. My problem isn't that I hate women, quite the opposite."

"Bullshit. Your interactions with women are almost exclusively sexual. Even our relationship, Shane. Despite the fact that we started out as friends and I care about you, haven't you noticed the ... shift?"

Fury was etched into his face. "What are you talking about?"

"You use women." She took a breath. "You use me."

"You feel used?" His tone, his very demeanor, was incredulous.

"You don't want to have sex with me. You need to. It's different. And coming out here with you, it's apparent. Between your mom and TruAchord. . ."

Shane stood and walked as far across the room from her as he could get—to the sink area outside the bathroom. "I'm sorry you've noticed me appreciating other women. I know some women can't handle it."

Amy held onto her temper with an effort. Of course he was defensive. "Stop trying to shift this onto me. Healthy guys in monogamous relationships don't check out every woman between eighteen and fifty. They just don't. I've had my share of relationships—"

"Oh they're checking them out. Maybe they're more subtle about it."

She considered his words. "Maybe. But that's the most obvious part, Shane. Your history is a nearly monogamy-free existence. All the problems you've had the last few years are based around women—even the issue between you and your brother-in-law."

He recoiled.

She watched the fury burning, a flush crept up his neck. "I can't believe you would throw *that* in my face. I was young and she was stupid. And you don't know Hollywood. You don't know what it's like, for an actor."

"Really? All celebrities have photos of their junk out there? All of them have trouble on set because they're sleeping with their co-star and members of the crew at the same time?"

He drew himself up, eyes sparking with anger. "That's not—"

"That's not what happened? Don't lie to me. I've got friends who worked at Enchanted but now work in Hollywood. Your reputation isn't all lies. And it isn't 'the women' out to get you. The common denominator is you."

He gaped at her. "I thought you knew me."

"I do. And I care about you. A lot. More than I expected to when I embarked on this thing. I wanted to keep things casual with you, but it's evolved."

"I've been faithful."

"Congratulations. That's the second time you've brought it up. Like you think you should be entitled to some kind of prize or …

or *medal*. We've never talked about it, but I'm faithful to you also. And it's no hardship, but it's not exactly smooth sailing for you, is it?"

"What's that supposed to mean? You have guys crawling all over you. At the rink, at bars, here."

"So? It's not like I'm tempted. Monogamy—fidelity—it's not a struggle."

He couldn't meet her eyes.

Her heart lurched. "Is it a struggle for you?" she said, softly, trying to keep the pain from her voice.

"No," he said. He strode forward and grabbed his keys, phone, and wallet off the bureau. "I'm going to go get us some lunch, then we'll get out of this shithole."

He slammed the door behind him.

Amy dashed away angry tears.

• • •

By the time he came back with two bags of Subway sandwiches and chips, Amy had all her stuff packed and was sitting on the bed, avoiding his eyes.

He tossed a bag to her, which she caught, but she didn't open. *Fine.*

His cell phone rang and he checked the number. "Goddamn it." He answered with, "Nat?"

"Shane? Have you left yet?" He could barely make out what she was saying, her words were so garbled by tears.

"No, we're checking out now. What's wrong?"

"He ... he left," Natalie wailed. "I threatened to do it without him with your money, and he walked out the door."

He closed his eyes and slumped, defeated. "Damn it, Natalie."

"We're both so exhausted, spiritually and emotionally from all the failures. From getting our hopes up for years, Shane. We've been doing this for an eternity and I … I want to hold a baby in my arms," she said, piteously bursting into a fresh round of tears. He gave Amy a helpless look and made what he hoped were soothing sounds into the phone. "Where'd he go?" Shane asked.

"Why?" she asked. "You can't talk to him. No one can reason with him. Either he has a baby with me or I have one without him. Even if I have to go to the sperm bank."

"Calm down, calm down. Okay? I'll stop over with Amy in a bit."

Shane disconnected the phone and started packing.

Amy came over to help, bringing his clothes, his toiletry bag.

All of this was his fault. He'd fucked things up for his sister, he was fucking things up with Amy. It never failed. His bad choices meant he couldn't help her. Why oh why hadn't he kept his dick in his pants seven years ago? He'd known how bad an idea it was to screw his married sister-in-law. He knew how immature she was. But in the heat of the moment, with all the stress of dealing with his mom, his dad's death, and the pressure of being the town's "favorite son," he'd needed an outlet that night. He was stupid and selfish and shortsighted. And Danica had thrown herself at him since he'd arrived in town.

Shane sat on the edge of the bed, everything packed around him, Amy in the bathroom. He heard the door open and close but didn't raise his head from his hand. His throat thick, he studied her perfect, pink toenails peeking out of strappy sandals on the beige carpet. He took a deep breath, ready to do whatever it took—beg if he had to, admit she was right—when her arms came around him.

Her palms smoothed through his hair and made long strokes down his back.

He took a shuddering breath and wrapped his arms around her waist. "I don't deserve you."

"I know," she said giving his hair a tug.

"Natalie threatened to use my money for the procedure. Jesse left her."

Her indrawn breath was loud in the quiet room.

He lifted his head from where it nestled in her warm, flat belly. "Talk to him," she insisted. "Accept responsibility. It was a boy who did those things seven years ago."

"You don't know Jesse."

"No, but I'm betting he's matured. And so have you. It can't hurt."

•••

Shane steered the rented sedan up the steep driveway to Miles Contracting. He parked and Amy gave his shoulder an encouraging squeeze.

Through the windscreen he spotted Jesse, in jeans, a tank top, and a Titans ball cap, wiping his hands on a rag, scowling at them.

He emerged from the car and hailed the other man.

Jesse jerked his head. "My office," he growled.

Jesse and Natalie had started dating their junior year of high school when Shane was a freshman. The oldest in a family of six kids, Jesse had been the man in his family after his dad left. He'd treated Shane like a younger brother, looking out for him. Jesse wasn't the first relationship his sister had, but he was the last. And how had Shane paid Jesse back? Screwing his kid sister in a coatroom, then later in his hotel bed. The next day she told a friend, who told a friend, and it was all over town and whispered in Danica's husband's ear before Natalie and Jesse had even left for their honeymoon.

By then they'd both realized how badly they'd messed up, but there was no going back. Danica was divorced and living with her mom six months later and re-married a year after that.

Guilt and shame didn't begin to cover it.

Shane leaned against the wall of the dimly lit office as Jesse settled himself into the chair behind the desk. "What the fuck do you want?"

"To fix this." He gestured between them.

"There's no fixing it."

"I know I made a mistake. A horrible mistake. I was stupid and immature—"

"From what I hear, nothing's changed there."

"—and so was she. And while it's fine that you continue to loathe me from afar, you're making my sister's life a living hell."

Jesse shot to his feet. "Me?"

"Yeah. I fucked up. Danica fucked up. What the hell does that have to do with you?"

"She's my kid sister and you wrecked her marriage. Now she lives in a trailer."

"She wrecked her own marriage. And from what I hear, she proceeded to wreck another one after that. So go ahead and blame me for the first one. I take full responsibility. I'll give you a crack at me. Take a swing. I won't defend myself." Shane took two steps forward. "But for Chrissakes, man. You have got to stop punishing my sister for loving *me* as much as you love your own."

His brother-in-law's expression was stunned. "I don't ... I'm not."

"You are." He sighed. "You made her choose a long time ago and she chose you, with my blessing. You won't allow me in your house. You don't go with her when she comes to see me. You make her feel guilty. You've been driving a wedge between us since you've been married. I've been paying the price for my folly for seven years and staying away, because I know how painful it is for her to know what you think of me." Shane gulped. "But you're making her pay that same price. And it isn't fair. This isn't about the money or your pride, it's about cutting off your nose to spite your face. Well, congratulations. Now we're all suffering."

Jesse stared at him, motionless.

"I've made piles of money, and my investor has turned around and made piles more. And if I can buy my sister a chance at happiness, I'll take it. Take fuckin' all of it, if it would make peace between us and give my sister the baby she's so desperate to have."

"I'm not taking money from you."

"Will you take a job? Build me a vacation property. A ten-thousand square foot house on Emerald Lake. I own a few acres out there. Will that work?"

Jesse was still scowling, but after a few seconds he gave a short nod.

Shane stepped back. "Great. My lawyer will send all the orders through."

"Why do you want to build there?"

"I love that lake. And I hope someday, if I have kids of my own, the cousins can go there in the summers."

Jesse looked struck. "You'd come back here?"

"Yeah. *If* we can put the past behind us. And if I can avoid Mandy." The two men exchanged a look of understanding.

Shane extended his hand across the desk and Jesse begrudgingly shook it.

When he walked out into the sunlight he was grinning ear to ear.

Chapter Fifteen

The black town car drove them back from the airport and pulled up to the curb in front of her house.

Amy grabbed for the door handle.

Shane had been contemplative on the flight home—probably because they'd had a male flight attendant. Something had shifted during the trip, and Shane had been noticeably more demonstrative—holding her hand, nuzzling her neck. She'd put up the armrest and slept on him most of the way home. But hovering over them was that fight, and the ride from the airport had been nearly silent.

She was happy to be home and get some space, get her head together—she needed to start adapting to her life without Shane. She'd be leaving in a few weeks and had to learn some changes to the Enchanted program at practice tomorrow.

The driver opened the curb-side door and deposited Amy's bags on the sidewalk before he helped her out.

Shane followed. "I still don't see why you can't come home with me tonight."

"I need to get some sleep and get prepared for practice tomorrow. There's only two more weeks until we go on the road."

"Can you give us a minute?" he said to the driver.

"No problem." The man got back in the vehicle.

Amy wrapped her arms around Shane's waist and leaned back. His expression was stony as he stared down at her.

"When do you move out?" he said.

"Kyle, Allyson, and I will be on the road by mid-September. We'll be putting our stuff in storage a day or two before we go," she replied.

"Will you move in to my place?"

"That's sweet, but it's only a few boxes and I'm sharing a storage unit with—"

"No. Will you move in with me? Now, today. I want you with me."

Amy's heart thundered in her ears. "Shane?" she said softly. "I'm leaving in sixteen days. I'll be on the road until May, with only a few breaks. I won't be living anywhere but hotels for the next eight months or so."

His gaze became searing, searching, trying to communicate something he obviously felt deeply.

She cocked her head. This was completely off the wall. After their fight in Tennessee and his "I don't do long-term" speeches when she'd first met him, she'd been erecting scaffolding around her heart for the inevitable breakup. And her heart needed the scaffolding, especially after what happened in Tennessee.

Amy pulled his arms away and took a step back. "I won't do the long-distance thing. I can't." Even if she did, she didn't think she could do it with him. "Wait. Are you asking me not to go on the road?" Her eyes narrowed.

"Of course not. I wouldn't ask or expect it. It's what you do. I may be on the road this year too if this role comes through."

"Then let's enjoy this while it lasts, okay?" She pulled his head to hers for a peck. But the peck turned into a slow stroking, and mingling breath. Amy pressed her body into his and felt the swell of his erection along her abdomen. "Shane," she murmured against his lips.

He put her away from him and knocked on the window of the car. The driver got out.

"Get my bag, would you please?" Shane exchanged the bag for a few bills. "Thanks, man."

"No problem." The man got back into the car and drove away.

He picked up her bag and stood smiling down at her. "Lead on."

"You want to stay here?" she studied him uncertainly.

"Yep."

No one was home when they walked into the stuffy house she shared. She led the way to her bedroom and opened her window.

Shane deposited her bag on the floor.

He took her in his arms, and, sweeping her up, deposited her in the center of her bed. He joined her, capturing her lips, his tongue sweeping over her lower lip.

"You feel so good," she murmured, her hands stroking his body shoulder to thigh, lingering to yank his hips hard against her arousal.

She opened for him, her tongue darting out to lick into his mouth. The hand gripping her waist tightened with near bruising force while the other slid up her thigh, slowly, teasing. The weight of him was delicious and she arched and moaned beneath him. And suddenly she was desperate, pulling at the hem of his shirt until he levered himself up with one hand and yanked the shirt off with the other. Amy shrugged out of the top of her dress, while Shane moved to the edge of the bed to shuck his pants and underwear and pull out a condom. Finally naked, he crawled over to where she knelt on the center of the bed, nude and shivering despite the warmth of the room. He stroked one shaking hand down the front of her body—stopping to cup one breast in his hand, long fingers toying with first one pebbled tip, then the other. His eyes were heavy lidded with arousal. She met his gaze, biting her lip to hold back a moan.

Never breaking eye contact, he ran the wide palm of his hand down over her stomach, as her muscles there twitched and fluttered. He slipped his hand over her and lightly flicked at her clit. She gave herself up to his hand as he teased, sliding one finger into her; her body clenched around it and he drew in a sharp breath. Another finger joined the first as his thumb circled her clit. She was desperate to pull him on top of her—to cease the torment and join their bodies. But there was something here, watching him pleasure her, memorizing every harsh plane of his face.

She wanted to kiss him, or close her eyes, anything to break the unbearable intimacy of this moment. Her body throbbed against his hand as his fingers continued to pulse into her body and he stroked her clit, waiting.

It was both arousing and mortifying that he was watching her, that he would watch her to completion. Her eyes widened, never leaving his as she bucked into his hand, trembling, coming with a low cry, boneless, exhausted, and self-conscious.

It was more than sex—it was unbearably intimate. Had she ever had an orgasm looking into her lover's eyes?

Shane rolled down the condom, shoved her lethargic legs apart and entered her with a thrust that pushed her body deep into the soft mattress.

She grunted in surprise, her body slick, but swollen from her orgasm, his rough entry almost too much.

He levered himself up on his arms, staring down at her, pumping into her furiously, almost angrily.

Amy wrapped her legs around his hips and surged up to meet his thrusts. His gaze moved to focus somewhere off to the left, on the wall. Oh no he didn't. If she could keep her eyes on him when she came, he could damn well look at her. She fisted a hand in his hair and brought his attention to her.

His eyes were wild and glassy, but they never left hers as he shuddered into her and came with a guttural groan.

He rolled his heavy, heaving body off her without a word and flipped over on his side, facing away from her.

Moments later she heard the long, slow breaths that indicated sleep.

Amy stared at the ceiling, fear knotting up her belly. What the hell just happened? That experience had opened doors she'd never looked behind. Brought in a level of intimacy she, with her plethora of short-term, intense relationships, hadn't experienced. Not even with Alexei, the Russian skater she'd fallen in love with on her third Enchanted tour.

She'd had sex with people she loved before, but this was something new and terrifying. And with a guy who told her he didn't do fidelity. A guy with disturbing attitudes toward women. She absolutely could not fall in love with Shane Marx. That would be disastrous.

Chapter Sixteen

A few days later Shane rolled over in his bed to spoon Amy. She stretched in his arms, groaning.

"You okay?"

"Sore from Enchanted practice the last few days. We're learning a new program," she said. "I'm happy to have the morning off."

"Hey, remember my attorney texted that he wants to see you this morning to sign some paperwork; he's figured something out with that endorsement money. He has something to go over with me as well, apparently. I missed a few calls from him when we were in Tennessee. Let's grab a bite and head over there," he raised his head to check the clock, "around eleven?"

"Sounds good," she mumbled.

Two hours later his attorney, Clay Langley, ushered Amy into his office. When she emerged thirty minutes later she appeared dazed.

"Shane," Clay's gaze bored into his. "You're next."

"You okay, Amy?"

"Yeah," she said, still looking out of it as she sat heavily in the chair beside him.

"Shane?" Langley said.

"Yeah, yeah," he muttered, standing.

Clay closed the door and Shane pitched himself into the leather chair closest to the door. Clay went to stand behind the desk.

"What's so urgent?" he drawled.

Clay rubbed his face. "Three days ago I got a letter from an attorney representing Kayla Clark. Does that name ring a bell?"

"Nope." Shane glanced at the door. Was Amy all right? She'd looked stunned. "Hey. What did you tell her anyway?"

"Who, Kayla?"

"No, Amy."

"Attorney-client privilege."

"C'mon man, I'm the one paying you."

"It doesn't work that way. I'm glad you sent her to me though. She'll tell you what's going on." He waved an impatient hand. "But your problem is a little more pressing."

Now the man had Shane's full attention. He liked this guy because he was so laid back—for a lawyer—but his voice was tense.

"What problem?"

"This woman, Kayla." The older man took a deep breath and looked away from Shane. "She's saying you impregnated her."

He bolted upright. "What?"

"Kayla Clark? Is she someone you've dated?"

Oh shit. Was this the girl he'd busted the condom on? Fuck. His stomach did a series of somersaults and landed in a pit that made him aware his breakfast may not stay down.

"Don't know her."

Clay stared Shane down. "So there's no possibility?"

He shifted in his seat. "I always wrap it, man. Always."

"Then there's no way this is a credible accusation."

"Well. . ."

His attorney peered over his glasses. "Well, what?"

"There was one girl, the ... the condom broke," he said in hushed tones, running a shaking hand through his hair.

"The condom broke? Was her name Kayla?"

He rubbed his face. "I don't know. We didn't ... get that far."

"Oh, Shane," the other man said sadly. "So this could be true? How long ago was this?"

"Early May?"

The man nodded. "This girl is about fourteen weeks along, give or take a few, her attorney says."

Shane picked at the seam on his jeans with trembling fingers. "So now what?"

"Now we request a paternity test. It used to be you had to wait for an amnio, but they can do a blood test on her—much less invasive—starting at about this time. And see if the DNA matches yours. You need to get to a lab for a blood draw."

His back pressed into the chair, putting as much distance between himself and his attorney as possible. "Seriously, man, it's probably not even mine. She took me home with her, but for all I know she could take half a dozen guys a week home."

"Well, let's hope so, but at any rate, we need to get our ducks in a row," Clay said matter-of-factly. "She'll want money, of course."

"Of course," he said bitterly.

"For the duration of the pregnancy."

"Aren't we getting a little ahead of ourselves? We're not giving her a dime unless we're sure it's mine. I'm damned sure it isn't," he insisted.

Clay's sigh was weary. "Sometimes it's best to err on the side of caution—in situations like these, when it's possible it's your child, you don't want to look like the asshole who didn't support her during her pregnancy. You look unsympathetic to a judge and it doesn't play well in the press."

"No. No fuckin' way. I will deal with all that once we know for sure it's mine." He forced the words out through a throat thick with fear. "If I pay her, it will look like I'm responsible." And what would Amy think? Best to assume some other guy knocked her up. "I'm serious. This thing is nailed down, I'll pay what I owe. But not until then."

"Shane, she's hired an attorney. She's got to be pretty sure—"

"I won't pay her anything until its certain."

"I'll get in touch with her attorney, she may have already had the test. You need to go to the lab this week. It'll be court ordered otherwise."

Shane stood. "That it?"

"Yeah. I'm sorry to be the bearer of bad news. She's a nice woman."

"What?" *A nice woman?*

"Amy," Clay said.

"Oh. Yeah, she sure is. Thanks."

He made an attempt to mask his horror from Amy when he returned to the waiting room, but she looked at him curiously nonetheless.

"You okay, Shane? You look … pale."

"Everything's fine. Now tell me what he said about your situation."

Her eyes lit up and she leaned toward him. "There *is* money, Shane. In a trust. My father finagled something with the people managing it—at least that's what Clay thinks. I haven't even received a statement. And I may owe taxes on it. There is something hinky going on, that much Clay is sure of. And given what my dad does, you know, that's not surprising. But it's sitting there, and it's been earning interest for seven years, Shane. *Seven years*," she whispered. "Clay thinks it will be a matter of signing a few documents, verifying some information, and it will be in my account by the end of the week. Can you believe it?" she said in hushed tones. "Clay says if I manage it well and try to live off the interest … and Shane, it's a lot of money."

Shane mustered a smile. "I'm glad."

Chapter Seventeen

"So this is it?" Shane dropped her bag at the entrance doors inside the terminal.

Amy bit her lip, nodding, willing tears away. She would not be the one to break down; she would wait until he left to weep, even if it killed her. It was a mistake to have him bring her to the airport, but he had insisted. She could tell he'd been preparing himself for this moment—he'd been distant since that meeting with the attorney. She would untether her emotions and the tour would distract her from everything, even a broken heart.

I'm getting everything I wanted, another year to figure out my life, another year doing what I love.

But the usual excitement she experienced going on the road was missing.

The breakup had been her decision. Shane accepted it with good grace, and he even agreed it was the right thing to do. He'd failed at the long-distance thing, too.

Shane raked a hand through his hair. "You've got everything?" He avoided making eye contact, his jaw tight.

"Yeah. Thanks, Shane. I wouldn't be here if it weren't for you. And keep up the practice, will you? Frank posts the open skate schedule online every week."

"I know," he said as he made a move to embrace her.

She backed up a step and held a hand up to stop him, swallowing back tears.

"Don't. Please. It's too hard," she said, gritting her teeth. She grabbed the handle of her bag, ignoring the hollow, breathless feeling as she blinked rapidly. Amy turned her back, pulling her suitcase behind her, and got in line for her boarding pass.

Silent tears tracked down her face, and the guy in line in front of her who'd been checking her out stared.

"Do you mind?" she hissed.

The man straightened and scowled, turning away to roll his bag to rejoin the line that had moved once again.

The tears continued as the line surged forward until she had to duck her head, wiping at her face.

She heard "excuse me" and patrons grumbling in line behind her. Probably some asshole late for his flight who thought he was entitled to go to the front of the queue. She looked up at the guy in front of her to see his expression register astonishment a split second before hands descended on her shoulders, turning her around.

Shane.

He pulled her hard up against his body. "I can't," he said, hoarsely in her ear. "I can't let you go."

"But we agreed—" She sniffed against his chest, burying her face in his familiar scent.

"Screw that. I can fly to see you. I've got nothing but scripts to read until my audition and who knows when that will be."

"This is a terrible idea," she said shakily, her arms wrapped tightly around his waist.

"We've both had bad experiences, but we can make this work. All I know is I want to be with you."

Her hands clutched him spasmodically. "Yes."

• • •

Shane adjusted his position on the yellow plastic seat and moved his feet, which were sticking to the floor. No surprise there, children surrounded him with their tubs of popcorn, drinks and cotton candy. They did this show twice a day? He'd meant to get in early, but he'd slept through his alarm, exhausted after last night's hockey practice. The amateur league he'd joined was turning out to be a lesson in humility. The next flight hadn't been until eight so he'd missed the first show.

He watched the vendors strolling the aisles with spinning light up toys, more soda and candy. He hadn't known quite what to expect, but he'd never been to anything like it. Children's voices raised with excitement. Parents were trying desperately to keep them in their seats in the interminable wait before the show started.

He tried to identify the feeling in his gut. Was it nerves? How could it be nerves? He'd seen Amy skate a dozen times.

The lights dimmed, the announcer's voice came over the PA system, and a hush fell over the crowd. It was astonishing how quickly the shrieking voices quieted.

A song came on—one he didn't recognize—and then a flood of skaters came out dressed as fairies, their costumes reflecting the spotlights, making glittery patterns in the ice. Their synchronized dance didn't last long because friendly looking furry monsters chased them, paired up, and danced. Shane sat forward on his chair, craning his neck for a glimpse of Amy.

The music ended and the fairies and their beast accompaniments disappeared from the ice.

Another song came on—this one a vaguely familiar love song— and there she was, in her skimpy yellow costume, heartbreakingly lovely. His heart hitched in his chest and then resumed its pace at triple the rate. He leaned forward enraptured, absorbed in her routine—the expression on her face, the joy in her movement. She whizzed by on one leg then danced in the spotlight, spiraling and leaping. He knew a few of the terms for what she was doing—a spin, now a double axel, nothing like she used to do, she told him.

He grinned. Even with the layers of makeup, her happiness was transparent. No wonder she didn't want to leave this. She was born for it.

Someone else entered the ice from backstage. Was that Kyle in a bright blue costume, dark wig, and tight, flared pants?

They skated toward each other and met in the center of the rink, where even from here he could see them gazing into each other's eyes. Jealousy rose up and he pushed it back down. They were acting for God's sake.

Then Kyle picked her up and his heart stopped. The man spun her, her blonde tresses flying out behind her. His heart resumed its erratic beat as Amy's skates met the ice again.

Another spin apart, more dancing together, backward this time before Kyle's stance widened and Amy leaned back—

Shane leapt to his feet.

Jesus, was that a death spiral?

Heart in his throat he watched Amy's head, inches from the ice, so close her hair swirled in circles on the frozen surface.

And that bastard Kyle leaned back, grinning, as she made three revolutions around the ice.

He was shaking, he realized distantly. And someone was saying something behind him, but he couldn't take his eyes off Amy.

After an eternity, Kyle pulled her up and they spun around the oval shape together.

Someone tugged on his shirt. A scowling woman said, "Sir, sit down. My son can't see over you."

Shane collapsed into his seat, heart thundering.

That looked dangerous. It was a death spiral all right.

He held his breath—now Kyle was lifting her above his head. So help him God if that man dropped her ... Shane stood again. And sank back into his chair as they embraced, both pairs of skates on the ground.

More backward skating, another lift. This time she was fully extended with Kyle holding her skates chest high. She moved gracefully above his head, bending over, her back arched until her head was hanging halfway down Kyle's blue suited back.

Shane was going to have heart failure if this continued much longer. A few more dancing embraces, one more hoist over Kyle's head, and the song ended with Amy draped across Kyle's lap. They left the ice and some other costumed creatures came on. The tension fled his body, leaving his stomach in knots.

God. He needed a drink. The vendor came by with a giant cup of lukewarm beer and Shane downed it with unsteady hands and bought another.

She came out three more times in different costumes, once with a prince who wasn't Kyle, but the moves they did were not nearly as daring.

He waited in his seat as most of the patrons shuffled out. His adrenaline had surged every time her skates had left the ice in a leap or jump, and now he was as drained as if he'd been out there on the ice, too. He wasn't sure he was in any state to go see her.

It was nearly twenty-five minutes later that Shane made his way to the backstage area where a security guard recognized him. "Hey man, you did a great job as the Avenger."

"Thanks," he said, shaking the man's hand.

"Enjoy the show?"

"You could say that," he muttered.

He spotted Amy still in her glittery blue costume, heavy makeup, and stockinged feet immediately. She was holding a Dixie cup full of something, likely champagne, and laughing with one of the sprites, or fairies, or whatever they were.

Her eyes met his and she grinned, still radiant, still on the adrenaline high from her performance. He remembered it well from his TruAchord days. He picked his way through the backstage area, over cords and equipment to meet her.

"What'd you think?" she asked.

He embraced her. "You were amazing," he said, softly.

She leaned back to look at him, clearly trying to puzzle out his expression. "But?"

"It was terrific—you were in your element out there and it was awe-inspiring."

She frowned. "Then why are you so ... off?"

He turned her around and slung a proprietary arm around her shoulder. "Introduce me to the cast," he insisted.

An hour later they said good-bye to her friends and made their way to the hotel he had booked.

• • •

Amy curled up on his chest, listening to the slow thud of his heart under her ear, her fingers lazily stroking his overheated flesh atop solid musculature. "So why did you look so strung out when you came backstage?" she murmured.

Instantly his heart rate picked up, until it pounded underneath her ear.

She sat up. "Shane?"

He pulled another pillow behind his head and she sat cross-legged next to him.

"I was pretty freaked out," he admitted.

"About what?" she asked, baffled.

"That routine. The lifts. The death spiral."

She stared at him, confused.

"It's dangerous," he insisted. "I've read about that move. It's called that for a reason."

She pressed her lips together to hold back laughter. The audience always worried more about that than skaters did. She hadn't given it a thought since she had absolute confidence in her partner.

He scowled. "It's not funny. It's hard to watch and Kyle. . ."

Her eyes narrowed. "This is about Kyle? I've told you he's a friend."

"No," his voice hardened. "It's about watching the person you ... care about ... get hoisted up and swung around over a hard surface. It's about fear," he admitted, taking her hand and encouraging her to lie back down against his chest.

"You don't think about it, do you?" he asked, softly. "How dangerous it is."

She turned his jaw until he met her eyes. "I'm a professional, Shane. It's not like I've never fallen or been dropped. And I have complete and utter confidence in my partner. I couldn't do this if I didn't."

"I know, Amy. But you have lasting injuries from falling and being dropped. We both know you do."

"I have some issues," she admitted. But it was more than that and the shows today—the first ones since May—had taken more out of her than she cared to admit. She'd been too nervous to eat since Shane was coming and despite being in such great shape, she'd felt breathless out there. Her hip was also bothering her more than usual. The jarring landings had put enormous stress on her hip for years. The doctor she'd seen to get an anti-inflammatory shot before leaving LA had spoken of arthritis and a hip replacement in her future. He'd been the first orthopedist she'd seen who had used that language and warned her that one bad landing or fall could mark the end of her career—if the problems from chronic overuse didn't end it sooner.

Chapter Eighteen

One month later, Shane paced in his lawyer's office. His phone vibrated in his pocket, and he pulled it out to check the incoming text. Not Amy. It was from a number he didn't recognize.

Fun night with u at Excel—Erika

He stared at the message, his heart racing with a combination of guilt and excitement. It was the brunette from last night's outing with his hockey team. Only one person had his cell number, the player-coach, Jason. That idiot must've given the girl his number after he left the bar. The guy had been so drunk by the time Shane left, he might not remember doing it.

He tucked the phone back into his pocket when Clay came to greet him.

He read nothing in the other man's expressionless face, but his heart raced, thundering in his ears.

They entered the office and Clay shut the door. Something told Shane he'd better take a seat for this news.

"I don't know what to tell you. She hasn't done the blood test."

"What? Why not?"

"I don't know. Maybe she suspects it isn't yours. Maybe she's planning to hose us in the press after the baby comes. Normally in these situations, they want the money coming in right away. Her attorney had the balls to suggest she'd get the test after they received a payment covering her medical bills and living expenses. I refused of course. That smacks of blackmail."

Shane scooted to the edge of the chair and held the armrests with shaking hands. "Can we force her? This thing is eating at me," he admitted.

Clay shook his head. "I've sent a letter basically telling him to either submit the blood work or withdraw the suit. Her lawyer says she's too busy or sick or whatever."

He snorted. "Bullshit."

"Either way, we can't compel her to do it yet. We'll have to wait and see. It's not the worst news, Shane. My gut is telling me she's hoping for money before the birth because she suspects it isn't yours. But it could be she's going to play it up in the media later to leverage more money. It's a toss up."

Shane raked a hand through his hair. "This fucking sucks."

"I know. Hang in there."

"I can't wait months for this thing to be resolved."

"She may drop it. You never know. In the meantime try to relax." Clay stood. "I'll keep you posted."

"Yeah," he mumbled. He tried to put this bullshit out of his head but the more he tried not to think about it, the more his brain looped endlessly around the idea of a stranger potentially carrying a life he would be responsible for—and what that would mean to him and to his relationship with Amy.

He needed to get laid. Maybe he'd fly out to see Amy. Where was she this week? Although he didn't want her to think he'd be there at every leg, and he'd just returned from her Baltimore stop. And he had practice two nights a week and scrimmages. The hockey club dictated his schedule these days, which he didn't mind. It was humbling to be outclassed by everyone from teenagers to sixty-year-old men. Humbling, but exhilarating. He was finally getting a chance to play a team sport, twenty-five years after he'd begged his mom to let him play soccer, and he didn't want to give up those moments.

Thirty minutes later, he entered his apartment and tossed his keys on the kitchen table. His phone vibrated again in his pocket—probably Jason responding to his text about not giving out his number.

I want your big hard dick in my tight wet pussy until you cum inside me baby (; -Erika

His breath quickened.

•••

Amy, Kyle, and a dozen others entered the glitzy bar, leaving the heat and humidity for the chill of the air-conditioned building on South Beach. .

"I love Miami," Kyle admitted as he followed the group to the back of the club. It was early and the place wasn't half full. One of the skaters had an uncle who owned the place, so whenever they were in town they hit Club Tropix.

Amy settled on the couch in the roped off VIP section and checked her phone.

Nothing from Shane, nothing all day. This was why she hated the long-distance thing. It required patience, trust, and a mellow attitude—three things she didn't have in excess when it came to him.

Kyle caught her and shook his head.

"What?" she asked, defensively.

"If you're not talking to or texting him, you're holed up in the hotel room reading. You don't go out. You used to be more fun," he complained.

"I'm out tonight," she returned calmly.

"Yeah, but only because you want to keep an eye on the perpetually drunk newbie, Jilly. You should've ended it, doll. The long-distance thing is not for the likes of us."

Amy powered her phone down.

Shane had been flying out twice a month to see her. And they'd been living it up in hotels, in restaurants and clubs with her friends all up and down the East Coast. Plenty of his friends joined, too. She'd met two of his TruAchord buddies, Gavin and Andy, when they'd flown in from New York to see her show in Virginia over the Thanksgiving holiday.

Shane was attentive and thoughtful and sweet when they were together. But when they were apart? He was a sporadic communicator, and that kept her on edge, insecure. There was a lot of time between shows and traveling between cities—plenty of time to obsess. She'd thought her life was back under control when Enchanted picked her up for this last season, and then when Clay Langley had discovered all that endorsement money. But nothing made her feel as unmoored as this relationship with Shane. And she still had no earthly idea what do with her life post-Enchanted if this really was her last season.

Four hours later, Tropix was packed and she was exhausted. They had two shows tomorrow; it was time to get back to the hotel. Jilly and Lisa, another skater, a veteran who had just ended a long-term relationship, were trashed.

"Kyle, I'm going to load these two up in a cab and take them back to the hotel." It was understood that the more senior skaters would keep an eye out for the junior ones. Amy herself had been in full rebel mode when she'd first gone on the road with Enchanted years ago. Fun as Rowena was, she was straight-laced. Going on tour the first time was akin to most eighteen-year-olds going to college. Kyle glanced over from where he toyed with a statuesque brunette's hair. "I'm not sure Jilly will be receptive to leaving," he said drily.

The skater was in the lap of someone she'd met early in the night, a well-dressed guy who had been buying their little group drinks. The two of them had been conducting a drunken romance on the couch, but the show was moving into X-rated territory as Jilly ground in his lap.

As the man came up for air he signaled for another round and Amy caught the glint of a wedding ring on his finger.

"Okey-dokey, that's enough of that," she growled, rising to her feet. "Excuse us a minute," she added to Kyle's sultry conquest, pulling him to his feet with one hand and grabbing her purse with the other.

She gave Kyle a push in the direction of Lisa and she moved to Jilly.

"Honey, come to the bathroom with me?" she asked.

Jilly gave her a drunken grin with a nasty edge. "Ooo, look, it's the princess."

"It is." She turned her gaze to the married guy under Jilly. "Will you excuse us a moment?"

Despite the drinks the man had put away, he didn't seen drunk. He narrowed his eyes. "Why?"

Amy gave an airy laugh and steadied the girl as she climbed off him. "I want to make sure she has everything she needs tonight," she replied with a broad wink.

"You want to make sure I have what I need?" He leered, rising from the couch.

Jilly pouted. "She's with someone, babe, and you have me." She tried to stroke the front of his expensive, pinstriped, button-down shirt but missed, tilting forward until Amy caught her around the shoulders.

"Bathroom," the girl muttered.

Amy steered her to the back, as quickly as she dared.

"I'm sick," Jilly said, staggering into a stall.

Amy followed, barely in time to whip the hair out of the girl's pasty face as she vomited into the toilet.

Could it be she was finally sick of this life? She had a responsibility to the younger skaters, but this tour she felt every minute of her age. Wasn't she was getting too old to hold someone's hair out of a toilet? Yet she'd been here with Jilly and others several times already this season.

The two women staggered out of the bathroom a few minutes later, Jilly apologizing. "I want to go home," she said tearfully.

"We'll go home," Amy soothed. "Let's get a cab."

"No, *home*. I've missed my brother's birthday and I'll miss Christmas," the girl wailed. "And they'll never make me lead princess. You'll *never* leave, will you?"

Amy stopped in her tracks in the hallway. Had Jilly been promised the lead? She had assumed Enchanted would eventually make Megan the principal due to seniority, but Jilly was a better skater. Was this why the girl was drinking so heavily? Guilt surged through Amy. It was past time for her to step aside.

The guy in the expensive suit she'd pulled Jilly away from stood at the end of the dimly lit hallway, the strobe lights from the dance floor lighting him from behind to give his figure a menacing aspect. Or maybe it was his shadowed expression, lips pressed into a thin line. From this distance he looked cruel and determined.

The hair on the back of her neck rose.

"She's sick," she said, taking a few steps toward him down the hall. "I'm taking her with me."

He didn't move.

Amy stopped and leaned Jilly against the wall. The girl slid down it, giggling. "You can see she's in no shape to—whatever." She made a gesture with her hand.

The man took two steps forward until he was in arms' reach. "I've been buying drinks for you guys all night. If you think I'm going to let you cock-block me, you've got another think coming." He jerked his head, indicating the exit door behind her. "You or her. My limo's out back."

Amy dug through her clutch. When she withdrew her hand, he grabbed her wrist, squeezing so tightly she yelped.

His eyes lit with excitement and he squeezed harder.

Eyes watering from the pain, her bones grinding together under the bruising force of his grip, Amy relaxed her face into her best innocent expression. "What? This?" She opened her palm and revealed a pink lipstick tube. Her expression turned what she hoped was coy and he let her wrist go with a grunt.

"Will I do?" she asked, stepping closer.

He pinned her up to his body. Her stomach churned as he hauled her hips against the erection tenting his suit pants.

Amy wrapped her hands around his neck as she pried off the stubborn top of the tube.

She raised her face to him. He leaned in, his eyes half closed. When he was two inches from her mouth, she leaned back, took a deep breath and held it.

Just before she depressed the spray directly into his face, she closed her eyes. She'd learned the hard way in Australia fighting off an overly amorous drunk at a backyard party that if she didn't they'd both be incapacitated by the mist.

He released her, roaring with pain, his hands clawing at his eyes. Blinded, he stumbled around in the hallway.

Jilly sat against the wall, muttering to herself, barely conscious.

"C'mon," Amy hissed, her heart thundering.

The man staggered toward them, fists rubbing his eyeballs, still bellowing, but it wasn't easy to hear through the club music.

She momentarily debated the exit door but remembered what he had said about his limo. Dark alley, potentially complicit limo driver. They were safer where there were more people.

She got Jilly to her feet and stumbled forward, half carrying the inebriated girl in the direction of the music. She wove the girl across the dance floor and to the exit.

Kyle was waiting outside, his arms wound around his date, kissing her and ignoring the drunken tirade Lisa directed at him. He raised his head at the sound of Jilly's whining, took one look at Amy's death stare and turned to the woman clinging to him, giving her a quick peck. "Maybe next time, babe. Tonight's not looking good."

The woman turned on her heel and strode back into the club without a backward glance.

Kyle stepped to the curb and hailed a cab. One stopped immediately and he helped get the two girls into the vehicle. They rolled down the widows, veterans at cab etiquette with drunks.

Kyle hopped into the front and gave the driver directions to the hotel.

Once they had settled the girls into their respective rooms, turning over their care to their long-suffering bunkmates, Kyle brought Amy back to his room—his roommate was still out at a club while hers was asleep.

"What happened?"

"I had to pepper spray him," she replied.

"Goddamn it! You should've come to get me."

"He approached us as we came out of the bathroom. He had a limo waiting in the back."

"I wish I'd been there."

"I'm tired, Kyle."

"Me too, Ames."

She hesitated. "Not that kind of tired—I mean, that too." She tried to sit cross-legged on the bed, but her hip had stiffened up. Instead, she pushed herself to lean back against the headboard. "I'm sick of it. Sick of life on the road. Sick of rescuing silly girls. I was so desperate to re-sign because I loved it so much—and I still love the skating, but the constant moving and the lack of privacy and … " And the pain. The pain in her hip was constant. Relentless. It was one thing to have a few bad hours after a show, but this tour she hurt every day, even when they didn't perform. The doctor had warned her that she'd have fewer periods of relief after the shot and he was right. She needed another. Tonight it was particularly bad, probably because she had spent part of the night hauling a drunk Jilly around.

Kyle took her hand. "I'm getting there myself. Are you going to leave the show?"

"After the chance they gave me? Hell no. But this will be my last rodeo."

"Are you hurting?"

She withdrew her hand. "No."

"'Cause if you are—"
"I'm fine."
"—your partner needs to know."
"I'm fine." She stood. "I'll see you in the morning, okay?"
Kyle walked her to the door.

Chapter Nineteen

Early the next morning, Amy took a long, hot shower, a thousand milligrams of ibuprofen and stretched, over and over. Nothing helped. She hadn't slept. The ache had become a stabbing pain, one that hadn't subsided during the night. She'd been here before, and the only relief came in the form of a cortisone shot.

She changed out of her yoga pants into jeans and a light top with a cardigan. Time to find an urgent care and beg for treatment. There was no way she could skate the program unless things improved dramatically.

Just as she was about to leave, someone knocked on her hotel door. She looked out the peephole. Matt, one of Enchanted's road managers, stood outside her room, scowling. Dread rose and Amy swung open the door.

"We need you down in the conference room. There's been a complaint."

"What kind of complaint?" she asked, coolly.

"The police are here and they're asking for you."

She closed her eyes. That guy from last night. He had money and entitlement written all over him.

"Corporate is flying in from Los Angeles," Matt hissed in her ear. "Looks like you pepper sprayed the wrong dude."

That did not bode well.

She turned on her phone to see she'd missed two calls from Shane. She didn't bother to play them; she didn't have time. Instead she texted him.

Trouble. Police here. Had to defend myself from a guy. Call you later.

Ten minutes later, she entered the conference room, outwardly calm, but inside shaky, hungry, and in pain.

At the table sat two uniformed police officers, a woman and a man.

Amy seated herself next to Matt, pressing her lips together to hide her grimace of pain.

"Miss Astor?" the uniformed man asked.

She nodded.

"A Mr. Trevor Dean came in this morning to make a report about your involvement in a pepper spray incident at Club Tropix last night."

She moved her hands from her lap to the table, threading her fingers together.

The female officer gasped, staring at Amy's arm.

Her sweater had ridden up, exposing her inflamed, bruised wrist. She tugged the sleeve down.

Both officers stared at her while she cast a nervous glance at Matt.

The male police officer stood. "Sir, would you mind stepping out of the room?"

Matt scowled. "She's my employee and we could be sued over this. My manager—"

The male officer indicated the door. "Out."

Once the door shut behind him, the officer resumed his seat. "Why don't you fill us in on what happened last night?"

Amy relayed the events of the previous evening while the officer took notes, his eyes boring into hers.

The female officer busied herself taking photos of Amy's wrist from every angle.

"I'm sorry for the trouble, Ms. Astor. Do you want to press charges?" he said, looking down at his paper.

"No. I think the less that comes out about this the better. My employer will be happier. What'll happen now?" she asked.

"Well, your injuries are consistent with your story—we'll interview Jilly, but if she was as intoxicated as you describe, it's doubtful she'll have much to contribute. We'll document what we've been told by each of the parties involved and make a report. It's unlikely Dean will pursue the assault charge, particularly in light of your injuries—if he does, it will go to the district attorney, who will determine the aggressor. Generally in cases like this, there will be a dismissal since you don't want to press charges, there were no witnesses, and frankly, the evidence corroborates what you've told us," he said.

The woman perched on the side of the table next to Amy. "Do you have any questions?"

"Can you let my employer know? I have a morals clause and this is the kind of thing they could use to force me out."

"I'll speak to the guy who was just in here." He handed her a white rectangular card. "If you or anyone from Enchanted Ice have questions, call. We're going to bring Jilly down for a chat. Thanks for your time."

She left the room and ran smack into Matt, pacing the hallway.

"Amy, I can't protect you from this. We can't have this kind of publicity. You'd best get your stuff together."

"I'm the victim here," she said stiffly.

"You think that'll matter? Trust me, it won't. I can't pull you off the ice today—not when we've got Lisa down with the flu."

Flu? Of course Lisa was in no shape to skate today, not after last night.

If corporate was coming out, if this Dean guy didn't drop his complaint, this could be bad.

She made her way down the hallway toward the elevators, careful not to let Matt see her limp.

Exhausted, she went back to her room, hung the do not disturb sign on her door, turned her phone off, and went to lie down and take the weight off her hip. Thankfully her roommate had already cleared out.

She'd get up in a bit and head to urgent care.

Amy woke up to a pounding on her door. She rose and limped over to the peephole. Kyle stood there, his expression tense.

"What are you doing?" he demanded. "The bus is leaving."

"The bus?"

"For the stadium."

Amy turned and looked at the clock. She gasped. "Holy hell, Kyle. I slept for four hours."

He helped her stuff her things into a bag and they dashed from the room.

• • •

Shane settled himself into the uncomfortable blue seat, a third of the way up from the ice. He'd wakened to Amy's text and immediately called Asher to ask to use his jet. He must've set a record getting from LA to Miami, and yet he still only managed to get there in time for the show. He debated going backstage but didn't want to distract her.

He leaned forward in his seat as the fairies disappeared, waiting for her appearance. She skated out, smiling, but even from this distance he could see her smile was forced, her jaw set as though she were gritting her teeth. Her skating was less graceful, less fluid. What was wrong with her?

Kyle skated out. Shane may have seen the performance a dozen times, but he still tensed every time that man appeared, as it signaled the start of the lifts and the dreaded death spiral. His stomach churned.

They spun by him, together, their steps perfectly matched, but Shane was close enough to see the grim determination on Amy's face and the stress behind Kyle's wooden smile.

Amy circled Kyle, preparing for the death spiral, but rather than tipping her, her partner spun her out from him, across the ice. Shane held his breath. That was not the move. Not unless the show had been re-choreographed.

They took another lap and he knew it wasn't his imagination— this was not the program. As they went back to the center, they spun and Kyle hoisted Amy in his arms, carrying her around the rink, her skates high on his chest. Unlike previous performances, she didn't drape herself over his back, but held herself stiffly in his arms.

The audience clapped and screamed; they didn't notice. But Shane had seen enough to know this one was way off.

Kyle released her, a move Shane had seen dozens of times. Amy spun in the air, two turns before the blade of her right foot met the ice ... and her leg crumpled before the other blade came down.

There was a collective gasp from the crowd.

Shane was already on his feet and in motion. He raced down the aisle, watching in horror as she went spinning, a full revolution on her rear, then bounced off her hip on the ice twenty feet from him. She tried to use the momentum from the fall to regain her footing but didn't make it to her feet.

Shane leaped over the rink wall onto the ice as she was getting awkwardly to her feet. He took two steps toward Amy in his street shoes and nearly landed on his ass. A man in a yellow windbreaker was shouting at him from the other side of the barrier; Shane ignored him.

She was up, fifteen feet away now, staring at him wide-eyed. She took one limping glide toward him and her face twisted with pain.

Slipping and sliding, but somehow remaining upright, Shane made his way to her. The only sound in the rink was the musical track still playing. The spectators were standing now, watching the drama unfold on the ice.

He was vaguely aware of Kyle, motionless several feet behind Amy, as he reached her.

The music shut off, the stadium was nearly silent.

Shane gathered Amy into his arms and the crowd burst into applause.

She held herself stiffly, and he whispered into her ear, "Oh my God, Amy, what is it? Your hip?"

She nodded into his chest; he wrapped his arms more tightly around her.

His mind raced. There was no way he could get Amy backstage without skates—even with skates he doubted his skills were up to it.

He looked around desperately.

Kyle met his eyes and came gliding over, stopping dramatically a foot away, his skates spitting ice.

Amy tugged out of Shane's embrace.

Then the man dressed as a prince reached for Shane's hand, raised it, then bowed as he released it, gesturing to the crowd for applause. The crowd shouted and cheered.

A dozen fairies skated out as the soundtrack started up again. They surrounded Shane, guiding him across the ice toward backstage.

He cast a glance over his shoulder in time to see Kyle sweep Amy into his arms with a flourish.

The crowd roared its approval as Amy forced a smile and linked her hands behind his neck.

Before he'd even left the ice he hissed to one of the skaters, "Get an ambulance."

"They're on their way," she replied.

"Has she been hurt, before tonight?"

The girl shrugged, depositing him in the area behind the curtain before she and the rest of the fairies departed to change for their next set.

Amy arrived backstage in Kyle's arms. He put her gently into a chair and still she cried out in pain.

Shane rushed over.

"You got this?" Kyle asked, his hand atop Amy's bent head.

"Yes."

The man departed, headed for the costume area.

Shane knelt in front of Amy, her face buried in her hands. Someone approached—a scowling man, Matt something, he'd met him before—and a gray-haired man in an expensive suit.

"Amy, what the hell?" Matt said, shuffling from one foot to another as his boss looked on. "You missed two jumps and the spiral—"

He rose to his feet, getting between Amy and this moron. "That's what you have to say? You walked over here to berate your skater because she's hurt?"

The man scowled and raised his voice. "If she was hurt, she shouldn't have been out on that ice at all. And you? Taking the ice in mid-performance without skates? Are you nuts?"

Shane took two steps forward and glowered down at the manager.

Amy raised her head. "He's right, Shane. I shouldn't have been out there. My hip is … hurt. I need to have it checked out."

The paramedics arrived, wheeling their equipment and stretcher into the cramped confines of the room. They helped her onto it—she cried out in pain and Shane's heart seized up.

He went over to unlace and remove her skates as one medic checked her vitals and the other asked questions about her medical history. Apparently she'd hurt it last night, hauling around an inebriated friend. The suit looked ready to blow a gasket. Matt kept asking for the name of the drunk friend, but Amy gave him a dirty look.

He handed his rental car keys to Matt. "Make sure these get to Kyle, tell him to bring her stuff. I'm going with them."

• • •

Three hours and one MRI later, the diagnosis was confirmed. Labral tear of the right hip.

The physician relayed the information in quiet tones and Amy burst into tears.

Shane sat next to her on the bed, enfolding her in his arms as she wept, her body intermittently shuddering and stiffening with pain. He didn't know what those words meant, but clearly it was devastating news to her.

"It's not necessarily a career ender, Ms. Astor," the ER doctor continued, "but it is a season ender. I have a call into one of our orthopedic docs who specializes in hips, and she can at least tell you options—surgery and the like."

An hour later the specialist arrived. She discussed alternatives and tried to allay Amy's fears. "You have options, Ms. Astor, and these days, there are alternatives to surgery. But whichever way you go, the process of recovery will take months. I'm sorry I don't have better news. There's a guy near where you live at UCLA who is very good. I can give him a call if you're interested."

"Yes, thank you," she replied dully.

Shane settled himself on the bed as Amy continued to cry quietly in his arms after the doctor left. He stroked her hair, helpless. "We can go home anytime; I have Asher's plane."

She nodded, sniffing into his shirt.

He looked up to see Kyle standing in the entry to the room, watching them expressionlessly.

"Labral tear?" he asked.

Shane nodded.

He released Amy, and Kyle came over to give her a hug and a kiss on the top of her head. As their eyes met, Shane was surprised to find he didn't feel a twinge of jealousy, only shared concern.

"Are you taking her home?" Kyle asked.

"Yes," he said, "as soon as possible."

"Good."

"And I'm siccing my attorney—our attorney—on the Trevor Dean situation," he added.

Kyle grinned and handed over the rental car keys.

"Chin up," the man told Amy. "Just last night you told me you were ready for a change."

Her tears continued to flow. "I know."

She leaned back on the bed and turned her face away, closing her eyes. Retreating into herself, leaving Shane helpless on the outside.

Kyle motioned him to follow him out into the hall.

"How bad is it?" Kyle asked bluntly once they had walked to the end of the corridor.

"Bad. Painful. The MRI shows a lot of chronic damage but also a significant tear. She's out for the rest of the season at least."

"Damn it," he said. "I hate that the decision was taken out of her hands, though she'd decided this was her last tour."

Shane raised both eyebrows. This was news to him. Amy had been desperate to be hired, and though she talked about life after skating, she seemed in no hurry to leave Enchanted.

"I'm debating how much to share with you about Amy. About how this might affect her—and her issues."

"The eating?" he replied calmly.

Kyle stiffened. "She told you about that?" he said.

"Yes."

"I'm not sure she's out of the woods there."

"From what I've read, you never are."

Kyle acknowledged this with a nod. "And lately ... well, I'm sure you've noticed that she's leaner?"

It was Shane's turn to freeze. Of course he'd noticed. He saw her naked every month, but Amy told him that was a natural consequence of performing. "She said it was normal to drop weight on the road, with how crazy the schedules are."

Kyle's expression was skeptical. "I've noticed the weight loss since I'm the one lifting her out there. She tells me the same thing. But I'm worried, and not just about the eating. I've known lots of skaters who've gone into a depression when they retire."

"That's what you think this is, retirement?"

"It should be," he said firmly. "And she knows it. The trouble with Amy—" His lips clamped together.

"The trouble with Amy is that she doesn't know who she is if she's not a skater," Shane finished his sentence.

"You get her, don't you?"

"Yes," he said. "And I experienced something similar when I left music."

Kyle shook his hand. "Then take care of her for us." He backed away, his expression serious before turning on his heel to disappear through the exit doors.

• • •

The doctors loaded Amy up on pain-killers for the flight home. Thank God they were going via private jet. It would make all the difference to her comfort. As they waited in the air-conditioned office in the Miami hanger for the plane to be readied for the cross-country flight, Shane's cell phone rang. He checked the number. Ike.

Amy was stretched out on the couch next to him so he got up and went outside.

"Hello?"

"Shane, you are a fucking genius, boy!"

One of the pilots nodded at him to indicate they could board.

"Ike, I gotta go."

"Sheer genius!"

"*What*, Ike?" He shouldn't have taken the call. Whatever it was could wait.

"Going out on the ice to rescue the princess? Brilliant move."

Shane frowned. "Move?"

"That video of your ridiculous self slip-sliding all over the ice to rescue your girlfriend is everywhere. There's a Buzzfeed of it! You are the man of the hour. Image problem solved."

"Whatever man, I gotta go."

"You coming back to LA?"

"Yeah. I'm flying back to LAX with Amy. Ike, the pilots are ready to take off."

"You holding up the flight?"

"Yeah, I'm on Lowe's Lear. I'll talk to you later."

Shane hung up, shaking his head. He couldn't give a rat's ass about his image when Amy was reeling.

· · ·

She slept most of the flight, though whether she was actually sleeping or in a narcotic induced haze could be debated. Shane read, looking over at her every few minutes until she waved her hand grumpily. "Stop checking up on me," she mumbled. "I can *feel* you worrying. I'm fine."

At the end of the flight, he hefted Amy into his arms. She'd definitely lost weight on the road. It had been gradual, but now, carrying her down the steps of the plane and into the private terminal, it worried him. She struggled in his arms to be put down. He did, afraid she would hurt herself otherwise.

She burst into tears when she couldn't make it two steps without gasping in pain.

Shane swept her up and carried her to the waiting limo cradling her shuddering body in the backseat.

Forty minutes later the limousine pulled up to his building. It was nearing midnight, but there was a swarm of paparazzi in the circular driveway.

Shane groaned. This was all they needed, some celebrity staying at his building. He was about to ask the driver to pull around the back when the horde spotted the car, and within seconds they were swarmed.

He stared in disbelief as thirty or more people in rumpled clothes with expensive cameras flashing, shouted his name and Amy's.

Amy stared out the window in shock.

"Fuck," he spat out.

She turned huge, dilated eyes on him. "Oh my God, Shane. I'm drugged and wearing sweatpants," she said in horrified tones.

He stared at her, then a bark of laugher escaped. He pressed his lips together, unable to prevent a grin.

He tapped the glass and the driver rolled down the window. "Let's make it quick, okay?" he said.

The driver agreed. He came around to let Shane out of the car, then got the bags from the trunk. Shane went around and scooped Amy up into his arms. She buried her face in his chest, and he couldn't resist dropping a kiss on the top of her shining gold head, ignoring all the shouted questions, the demands, the strobe-like lights of so many cameras going off. The swarm stayed outside, and the door to the lobby shut, leaving them to wait for the elevator in relative quiet.

"What was that all about?" she asked, squirming to be put down.

"I'm not putting you down, so stop wiggling."

He entered his apartment, put Amy on their bed, and went out to tip the driver, who left their bags at the front door.

Amy was sitting on the bed, feet up, when he returned. He unlaced her sneakers and checked his watch. It was time for another dose of the pain meds. He got her pill and some water.

She took it begrudgingly.

Shane checked his voicemail—a million messages from his sister to his agent. He ignored all but the one from UCLA Medical Center. "The orthopedist will see us first thing tomorrow. 10 A.M.," he relayed.

"Shane," there was trepidation in her eyes, "what was that all about? Outside? Has something happened?"

He saw what she was really asking; she wanted to know if he'd done something, gotten caught. "Ike called while you were sleeping. He told me there's video of us online, of what happened on the ice in Miami."

Her eyes widened. "There is?"

"Yeah, and he's excited. He probably sicced the media on us." He shook his head, lips twisted. "Which is the last thing you need."

"Lemme see," she slurred, her pupils swallowing up all the blue in her eyes as the pain medication took effect.

He grabbed his iPad and did a search, pulling up an *Entertainment Today* story on it. He sat next to her on the bed, watching the model turned reporter give their backgrounds, load in a bunch of supposition about their relationship, and then the clip. The footage looked professionally shot. It picked up where he got to the rail and hopped over, focusing on him, not Amy, on the ice.

This was no amateur shooting on their iPhone. This was Enchanted's camerawork. They had put this out there. The camera operator went in for a close up as Shane made his way across the ice, revealing his expression, tortured and stark.

It was all there.

He sat, immobilized, staring at the screen.

Amy turned shocked, glazed eyes on him.

"Shane?" she asked.

He turned his gaze from her back to the footage—the camera tracking her as he took her into his arms.

Kyle stood impassively a few feet away, letting thing play out like the showman he was.

The video ended and they cut back to the anchor, who raved about the romanticism of the moment and the awkwardness of being on ice without skates.

They'd captured what he'd been so careful to hide, his heart shining out of his eyes, and they had put it out there for millions of people to see. To use to sell tickets.

"Shane?" Amy said again, softly, a tear slipping down her cheek. She took a sobbing breath.

He said nothing, his heart racing, thundering along. He tilted his head and pressed his lips to hers gently, carefully, despite everything, still struggling with the words.

Chapter Twenty

Amy barely leaned on her cane as she led the cameraman down the long, dim hallway to the place dubbed the "kiss and cry," an area reserved for figure skaters to revel or sob over their performances. All the triumph and heartache displayed for an audience.

Immediately after the fall and the publicity over her injury and love affair, Ike had taken her on as a client. Four weeks after her arthroscopy, her hip was significantly better. Nowhere near normal, but she could move and sleep without pain. She swam every day and had done PT right up until yesterday when she'd flown from Los Angeles to Boston for this gig Ike had gotten her: commentating for the broadcasting network at the Figure Skating Nationals.

If all went well, they wanted her to interview skaters for the Olympics, too. The money was excellent. And Ike had high hopes for her post-Olympic career. Amy didn't have the heart to tell him she wasn't going to act or do reality television or whatever else he envisioned. Thanks to the half million dollars of endorsement money Clay Langley had dug up, she didn't need a television career of any kind.

Shane had been dead set against the job. He wanted her to focus on her recovery in Los Angeles. They'd been living together since the return from Miami and she'd never lived with a man before, not as his lover. She'd also never had anyone take care of her the way he did before and after the surgery. Shane had risen to the occasion, he put up with her moodiness, pain medication that apparently made her loopy and sexually insatiable, and her finicky appetite. It was a different kind of bliss. She couldn't have asked for a better person to shepherd her through the surgery and rehab and schlep her to and from doctors' appointments. She could see he worried about her decision to commentate at Nationals, but he'd given in with good grace. She needed to start down the new path. Oh, the irony of that conversation with Kyle back in June, no coaching, no commentating. Life had made a mockery of her plans this year.

This was it, the last qualifying competition prior to the selection of the U.S. Olympic figure skating team. It was a pressure cooker of an event.

Things had changed since she had been at this very competition all those years ago. The programs were more difficult for one thing. There would be no surprises, no dark horse. The event was a formality because coaches and judges had their favorites; the team was all but set in stone.

Giant winged birds swooped in Amy's stomach. It wasn't just the nervousness of being on network television and fearing she would make a fool of herself. *She* was here. Her nemesis. Yarotska.

Amy was jumping out of her skin.

Her cameraman, Chris, looked over at her.

"You okay?"

"Fine." She attempted a smile through stiff lips.

"You're going to have to do better than that," he said with a dubious expression, hitching the heavy camera higher on his shoulder.

She searched her mind for a mantra, rolled her shoulders, and took deep, calming breaths. Nope. Not helping. If only Shane were here to give her a pep talk. Or Rowena.

The music started, indicating the first ladies figure skater was taking the ice.

While two figure skating legends critiqued the performances during the program, Amy would interview them afterward as they craned their necks at the screens above for their scores. And the live cameras would capture the scores—those intensely personal revelations of success or failure—with its unflinching eye.

By the time the third skater left the ice, she had done her best to interview two girls who had skated flawlessly, though the judges scores didn't reflect their efforts, and one nearly perfect performance from a young woman guaranteed a spot on the team. Nothing new there. The sport had a long history of behind the scenes deal making in national and international competitions. Judging scandals and a flawed scoring system plagued figure skating.

The fourth skater, top-ranked Becky Miller, was out on the ice. She watched the eighteen-year-old athlete. She'd seen Becky skate many times over the years, and if she could have a favorite, this girl would be it.

She had clawed her way from poverty and obscurity to train with the elite solely based on her grit and athleticism. But watching her now, Amy couldn't believe this was the same girl who placed third in the world championships last year.

This was Yarotska's protégé and the top selection for the U.S. team? The girl was skating an incredibly conservative short program and while she hadn't missed any landings, there were a few wobbles. Maybe she was afraid to risk injury since the Olympics were only a few weeks away.

Becky made her final pose as the music faded out.

"Showtime," the cameraman muttered as Amy stepped forward to greet the girl coming off the ice. Someone brushed up against her, the scent of cigarettes and an unforgettable noxious perfume stirring old memories to life. Yarotska. Amy straightened her spine and greeted Becky with her princess smile glued to her face.

The girl murmured hello and gave her a limp handshake before dropping herself next to her coach.

The skater looked exhausted, her sunken eyes accentuated by the makeup, face beaded with sweat, chest heaving. Amy seated herself next to the skater gingerly, her smile fixed, microphone at the ready. She could hear Diana and Burt, skating legends, discussing the performance in her ear-piece. They were straining for positive things to say about such a lackluster performance. Like the coach, Amy automatically craned her neck at the monitors, awaiting scores, as she had so many years ago.

She glanced at the girl next to her, but rather than looking for her scores, Becky was staring into space. While Amy watched, a startled expression crossed the skater's pale face, her eyelids fluttered, and she slumped, her body pitching forward off the wooden seat and onto the floor.

Amy gasped. She dropped the microphone as she instinctively went down to the girl. Her coach spared the girl on the floor a glance, but went back to gazing at the monitors as the voice droned the numbers.

"Amy," the camera man hissed.

She looked up at him. "Get a medic."

He remained motionless, continuing to film. Amy glared at him. Looking past Chris, she spotted a few people with badges. "Get someone!"

They scurried away, and satisfied they would get help, she turned her attention back to the skater.

The girl was pasty white now, hairline damp with perspiration. Amy helped put her limbs in a more comfortable position and moved her onto her side in case she was going to throw up. With a long moan, the girl started to come around.

"Mom?" she bleated, casting about the area.

"Becky, you're okay. You fainted."

"Feel sick," the girl mumbled. "Dizzy." Her hand went to her head.

Martina Yarotska still hadn't moved from her position on the bench. "Champions don't give in to the pain. Get up Becky," the woman said.

"Rest," Amy contradicted, glaring at Yarotska.

"Mom?" the girl said, again, struggling to rise with tears tracking through her cosmetics.

Amy put a hand on her shoulder. "Becky, stay down until the medics come check you out." The girl was panting, her heart racing inside the too thin chest. Amy's gaze swept over the slender body, examining her critically. No wonder she was having trouble with her performance—up close the girl looked too thin; she had lost that athletic build since last year.

"You did this, didn't you?" she hissed to Yarotska. "You took this beautiful girl, this virtuoso on skates, and pushed her to this, didn't you?"

"Ah," her former coach said, loudly. "The failure speaks."

The girl at her knees tried to push herself up, fear evident on her face. "Coach Yarotska?"

The beady eyes stared down at the girl on the floor. "*Da*. Get up, child."

"What have you done?" Amy whispered. But she already knew. No wonder Becky had skated so conservatively. She probably didn't have the energy for the most complicated jumps.

The paramedics arrived and loaded the girl onto the stretcher. They asked Amy a few questions before they pushed her through the crowd that had gathered.

And the entire time, a burning anger smoldered inside her until she couldn't ignore Yarotska's pretense that this was only a momentary weakness on Becky's part. "You've made her anorexic, too, haven't you? With your weigh-ins and your bullying." Her voice rose. "It's not worth it, nothing is worth her health. Certainly not a medal on a podium."

The coach rose from the bench; she was short but stocky and stood too close, trying to intimidate.

Amy stood her ground.

She pointed a finger, nearly touching Amy's nose. "You know nothing, you spoiled girl. You *failure*. I make world-class."

Amy leaned right up in her face. "So that's what we all watched just now? World-class? *God.* Nothing ever changes, does it? You drive these desperate girls to starve themselves, to work out until they bleed, to skate with fractures. You sicken me."

Amy turned away and spotted the nearly silent crowd that had gathered to watch.

She made her way to where the swarms of people were outside the exit and stood before the white rectangular doors of the ambulance. She knocked.

A medic opened the door and saw her standing there. "No interviews," he barked out.

Realizing she was still wearing an earpiece, she ripped it off and threw it onto the ground. "I'm not here as a reporter. I'm a former skater and I'm worried that she won't tell you what's really wrong here. "

The blue uniformed man opened the door wider. "In that case come in. Maybe you can give us some answers about what's going on."

Amy sat on the bench and watched Becky, already hooked to a heart monitor, an oxygen mask strapped to her face. The other medic was starting an IV.

She looked away, squeamish.

"Can you give me any history on her? Her parents haven't made it down here yet. They were in a skybox. Does she have any chronic illness? Using performance enhancing drugs?"

"All I can tell you," she said softly, "is that when her coach was my coach, the woman encouraged me to starve myself. I collapsed after an event and had to be taken to the hospital with an erratic heart rate."

The two medics exchanged a look, then they all stared at Becky, whose tears were sliding down her cheeks, making rivulets around the oxygen mask.

"I was low on protein and my electrolytes were dangerously off—I don't know specifics. It took the doctors a while to figure out what the problem was. I wasn't honest about what was happening. . ." Her breath hitched and she corrected herself, "About what I was doing to myself."

The medic turned to Becky. "Do you want your coach or parents to ride with us?" he asked.

Becky silently shook her head and pointed a finger at Amy.

"She's eighteen," the female medic piped up, "and I've got this IV started. I'm not a huge fan of what I'm getting on the monitor," she said calmly, with another meaningful glance at her partner. "Let's go."

They arrived at the hospital in a matter of minutes, only to find a swarm of reporters parked outside the emergency room and an overwhelmed security guard.

The doors opened and the mob of people surged forward, blocking the entrance. The medics lowered the stretcher.

Reporters were shouting her name, Becky's name, and, bizarrely, Shane's name. Four police cars pulled up and half a dozen cops hopped out to do crowd control. Amy ignored the microphones pushed at her as she followed the stretcher. Becky waved Amy closer with eyes wide and terrified above the oxygen mask. While they waited for a room in the hallway, Amy took the hand without the IV and gave it a squeeze.

She bent over. "You're going to be okay, Becky."

But was she? It had taken a year of therapy to get her head anywhere close to right after she and Rowena had fled. And the disease was still there—the mindset never completely went away. *Regain control*, it whispered, *control the food and workout.*

Her cell phone rang continuously while she waited in the curtained area with the young skater. She hadn't forgotten about her job, exactly, but this was more pressing. The emergency room nurse gave her a dirty look and she switched it off. Whatever it was could wait.

The nurse changed the IV bag and took vitals while the medics unhooked their equipment and switched over to the hospital ECG and oxygen.

Finally, the two medics wheeled the stretcher away, but not before the uniformed woman reached out to touch Amy on the arm. "Good luck," she said quietly.

Ten minutes later the nurse left and the white-coated emergency room doctor came in and pulled the curtains behind her. "What a zoo," she remarked. "Young lady, your parents and coach are here—they're out in the hallway and insisting they be let in to see you. Do you want me to send them in?"

Becky bit her lip, her gaze downcast.

"I guess," she said.

Amy held in a sigh.

The doctor's gaze was steely and directed at Amy. "The medics filled me in, but we see this occasionally—and the blood work speaks for itself. Don't worry," she said in her clipped but friendly fashion, "there's only so much bluster and denial we'll allow." She switched her stare to Becky. "This is serious business, young lady, and we need to know what is going on in order to figure out how to help you. Do you understand me?"

"Yes," the girl on the bed whispered.

"I'll make my recommendations once we have more information from your labs. Is there anything you want to tell me now?

The girl shook her head, but her eyes pleaded for something.

The doctor signaled to Amy. "I need you to step out while I try to get to the bottom of this."

She leaned against the counter outside the curtained room. Almost immediately the Millers and Yarotska walked in. Mrs. Miller glanced at the curtain, heard the sobbing.

"Becky?" her mother entered the room, closely followed by her husband and the coach.

Five minutes of eavesdropping taught her that Becky was not made of stern enough stuff to face down her parents and Yarotska, or she wasn't willing to admit what she had been doing.

"Exhaustion," Mrs. Miller insisted. "She's training too hard. Could happen to anyone."

"Dehydration," Yarotska's heavily accented voice put in. "No problem."

Amy grew angrier and angrier as they cajoled and bullied the girl into saying she was ready to rest to prepare for the Olympics. And of course she couldn't give up now.

Thank God the doctor wasn't buying it. "I'm concerned about a number of things. There's the fainting, and your child is significantly underweight."

"She's a champion figure skater," Mrs. Miller said.

"Her heart rate is abnormal and I'm waiting for the labs. At the very least she'll be kept overnight for observation," the doctor said.

"Fine, fine," Mr. Miller's voice came through the curtain. "She'll be fine. She's exhausted, training too hard."

"Yah," Yarotska agreed. "We will taper now."

"Becky?"

There was a long silence.

"Becky?" the physician said. "If this is more than exhaustion—and looking at you, looking at the monitor, I suspect this is more than that—you need to understand that starving yourself could cost you more than your figure skating. It could kill you."

"I'm fine," the young girl said, so softly Amy could barely hear her. "I'm tired. I need to rest," she pleaded and started to cry again.

The doctor left the room, shaking her head at Amy.

"You can't let them do this," she hissed. The doctor glanced around and pulled her into a staff area.

The woman stared at her, compassion evident. "In my business you learn the hard way that you can't save people from themselves. They have to want to fix their problems, make the changes. She's eighteen."

"So what? You have a responsibility—"

"I can't have her committed for an eating disorder—not at this point. And even if her parents were in agreement that she needs treatment, it doesn't work unless *she* wants to help herself. I suspect you know this," the doctor said, giving her a hard look.

"I've had similar struggles," she admitted.

The woman touched her on the arm. "Then I don't need to tell you this is a battle no one can fight for you." With that, the doctor left the room.

Amy wandered to the waiting room.

A man wearing a network badge approached her.

"Amelia?"

She sighed. "Yes?"

"There's a meeting in the conference room a few doors from here. I've been asked to bring you over."

The producer was in the room, pouring a coffee into a Styrofoam cup. He put the cup down when she entered. "Amelia!" he greeted heartily. "We only have a few minutes until the skating people get here." He pulled her into a corner and whispered, "Did you get an exclusive? Will she be agreeable to an interview with you?"

Amy frowned. "I'm sorry, what?"

"We weren't too thrilled when you dropped your mic, but then you went toe to toe with your coach and we got some great footage. The blogosphere is all abuzz speculating on the real story, your history, her history with Coach Yarotska. Is Becky anorexic? Are you?" He couldn't mask the excitement in his voice.

Nausea rose up, the sour taste of bile in the back of her throat. This was some kind of ratings bonanza for them.

"We need to nail something down," he continued. "The figure skating world is going to come down hard on us to bury the real issue here," he rubbed his hands together, "but there's nothing they can do if we get an exclusive with her."

The door opened and three members of the U.S. Figure Skating Commission entered the room.

They were all staring at Amy.

"She won't talk about it—about anything," she told him loudly.

Relief was evident on the faces of everyone in the room except the two network people.

The producer's hand tightened on her arm. "What do you mean?" he said in an under voice. "I thought we'd have an exclusive."

Amy wrenched away. "No." She pulled her ID badge over her head and threw it on the table. "I'm done."

She returned to the waiting room—the physician had said they would have to admit her to get her heart stabilized. Once her coach left, Amy would make one last ditch effort to talk to the girl.

Chapter Twenty-one

Where the fuck was she?

He ordered another drink at the bar. Practice had run late tonight, but eight of the guys on his team had browbeaten him into going to their usual hangout, Excel. He'd called twice and texted four times since late afternoon. Nothing. Thirty minutes ago he'd called the front desk of her hotel and told them there was a family emergency. The hotel sent a bellhop up to her room at 2:30 A.M. her time, but there was no answer to the knock. She wasn't there. She hadn't contacted him.

His gut twisted. Maybe she was out. Did he think he was the only one who did that?

Shane pocketed his phone and finished his drink in two swallows.

He looked down the bar to where his friends were flirting with a group of women.

He pulled a few bills out of his wallet to cover his tab and spun on his seat—right into a gorgeous brunette with almond-shaped eyes and lustrous tanned skin.

Erika.

His heart raced as adrenaline and excitement surged through him.

She looked him up and down, supremely confident, her gaze assessing. She put her drink down on the bar and took his hand.

Her fingers were long, her palm wide, and he could feel the bones prominent beneath the surface.

She led Shane down the dimly lit hall and he followed to an emergency exit.

Before he'd even finished backing into the alcove, the thrill was dissipating. Adrenaline gave way to anxiety, his stomach roiling. He pulled her into his arms—she was all sharp angles and overpowering musky scent.

He ignored his stomach.

She lifted her mouth for a kiss, but he nuzzled her neck instead, unable to bring himself to kiss those pouty, shining lips. He was rock hard as his body ignored the message his brain was sending: abort. He spread his legs, pulling her body between them, his hands taking her protruding hipbones and rubbing her against himself.

Her lips sought his again so he ducked his head, feigning interest in her chest. It wasn't right. There was too much of her and not enough all at the same time. The smell was off. It was all wrong, but still his body drove him, desperate for an escape from his own head.

He never stopped rubbing her hips against his, stroking himself through his clothes. His hands went to the hemline of her short skirt, he slid it up, and cupped her narrow, bare ass. She made a sound. Excitement? Half-hearted protest? He didn't know and didn't care.

Her sticky, hot lips were insistent on his face, and he avoided her kiss for the third time, averting his head.

A rustling sound, a footstep, alerted him to their discovery and he lifted his head from her neck.

• • •

The knock came as Amy was closing her suitcase.

She nervously glanced toward the door. Ike had called at noon to let her know she'd been released from her contract. He'd made her aware of her options—warned her that the word was out and the network was already getting flack for letting her go.

She stepped up to the peephole and examined the man standing in the hallway. Sunglasses, hat, and some high-end teal ski jacket. Duffel strapped across his broad chest.

Shane.

Amy flung open the door and launched herself in to his arms. He returned her hug and with a final glance down the hallway, pushed her into the room.

"Are you okay?" he said, his voice full of concern. "I'm sorry I wasn't with you. I can't imagine how hard that was, with Yarotska and Becky."

"You know?" she said, softly.

"Babe, it's all over the place. Ike told me *Morning in America* aired footage. Lots of reporters downstairs in the lobby," he said. "I came in through the kitchens."

She pulled the hat off his head and wrapped her arms around his neck, urging his mouth to hers. She didn't want to talk, not now. He yanked her tight to his body, holding her up against him. She stared into his blue eyes, hot and heavy lidded with desire. His face was rigid, intent, tense. Then his lips met hers and she stopped thinking at all.

His kiss tasted of urgency, of desperation. Amy leaned back but he followed, hungrily, his tongue licking into her mouth, backing her into the bed.

She moaned her pleasure as her tongue met the slick, wet thrust of his. Shane's hands locked her mouth to his, spinning her out of control.

She whimpered as his mouth left hers to explore her neck, leaving a burning trail of sensation. She felt his body bow with tension as it pressed against her knees to chest; his hands swept down her body, grinding her hips urgently against his.

Her hands slid down to the muscles in his shoulders, stroked over the ridges of his abdomen. She pushed his jacket off his shoulders, lifted his shirt and sweatshirt and laid her head on his chest, panting, reveling in the sound of his thundering heartbeat.

His body shuddered in her arms. He pulled away only to yank off his layers of clothing, his hands visibly trembling. She stripped off her shirt, shucked her cotton leggings, removing her panties in the process until they were both naked, breathing hard, staring at each other next to the bed. She explored his thickness, her hand wrapped partway around his pulsating hardness. She squeezed him, once, hard, and he made an anguished sound. He moved her back until she was sitting on the edge of the bed and pulled a foil wrapped condom from his jeans. Amy took it from him and rolling it over the engorged flesh, she glanced up at him. He was staring down at her, his cheekbones flushed with arousal, lips compressed into a thin line, but it was his eyes that held her attention. His gaze was focused and intent, more than passionate—

"God, Amy," he said hoarsely.

She encircled him with both hands and tightened her fists, delighting as his expression changed to one of exquisite, painful pleasure and he cried out, surging into her hands. But his hot blue eyes were still locked on her, not on her hands, not her breasts, watching her.

The ache of desire had become an insistent throb.

She laid back onto the bed and spread her legs. One long finger trailed up her inner thigh. She shivered and shifted restlessly as his fingers moved to her cleft where she pulsed, slick and aching.

"Shane," she pleaded. Her hand at his shoulders urged him to her, desperate. "Please." He gentled her with a deep kiss while his clever fingers stroked, coaxed, knowing how to make her gasp and beg.

Her body shifted restlessly on the bed.

Amy arched her back, eyes riveted to his. Slowly, so slowly, he pushed the broad head of his cock against her, rubbing and stroking her. Teasing. She pressed down, frantic to have him inside her.

He resisted her and continued the slow, inexorable press forward, entering her, stretching her, making her wild. She raised herself up to accommodate him, ignoring the twinge of pain in her hip. His blue gaze was fierce, he panted, giving her the time she needed to adjust to his size. Her hands went to his hips and she clenched them, urgently, their eyes still locked as he withdrew, then started forward again as her hips rocked. He thrust all the way in and she let out a long, thready cry. His movements became more frenzied.

He groaned his pleasure into her; she raked her nails down his back as he stroked in and out of her, establishing a relentless rhythm. She came with a long, thin wail, swept over the edge as he made a final thrust and came with a hoarse shout of his own.

She curled up into him and closed her eyes, able to feel his body slacken as sleep took over him.

Amy propped her head on her arm and watched his face, that ridiculously beautiful face, completely relaxed and unguarded for once. She had no idea how long she lay there, watching his mouth slacken, the slow deep breaths of sleep, but her hip was tightening up after all that activity and the physical therapist had given her some exercises to do when that happened. With a sigh, she slid carefully out of the bed, pulled on her leggings and shirt, and went into the suite.

She cast a disparaging glance at her purse. Her messages couldn't wait forever. Kyle would want to know what was going on. She settled onto the loveseat with her phone and stared at the screen. There were two dozen missed calls—a bunch from Shane, two from Ike, one from the network, and several from Kyle. It would be faster to answer text messages. Six from Kyle asking if she was okay from last night, then the final text.

Have you seen the photo? I'm worried about you. Call me. NOW.
Oh God. Please, God, no.

She opened the browser. Typed in his name. Two clicks later, she couldn't catch her breath as she stared at a photo of Shane and the hiked up skirt and bare ass of the brunette in his arms. The gossip site told her all she needed to know—when, where, who. Everything but *why*.

• • •

Shane awoke disoriented. He moved his hand to her side of the bed. Cold. He must've fallen asleep after they had sex.

"Babe?" he called. "Amy?"

He hopped out of bed and put on his boxer briefs. Yawning, he made his way to the door to the suite living room where Amy sat huddled up on the couch, pale, and avoiding his gaze.

He stepped closer. "Amy?"

"Is there something you want to tell me?"

There was something wrong with her voice. It sounded thick.

"Hey, are you okay?" He crossed the room to her and she held up a warning hand.

"Shane, I'm giving you. . ." she took a deep shuddering breath, "a chance to explain yourself."

She still wasn't looking at him.

He backed up a step, a mass of writhing anxiety in his belly. "What?" Crap. Was that paternity shit out there now? His attorney told him the baby was due any day—when was that? Last week? Where was his damn cell phone? He spied it on the table a few feet away. Fuck. He must have missed a call from Langley. Probably several from Ike.

"*Shane.*" Now she was looking at him, her hand covering her mouth. "I think I'm going to be sick," she whispered.

"Some girl says I fathered her kid. It's all bullshit," he said, trying to make his tone even.

Her head cocked, her face remained expressionless, and she still was not looking at him.

He couldn't get a read on her.

"A paternity suit?" she said softly but with a hard edge.

His gaze moved around the room. "It's nothing. The baby isn't mine. I took a test." That was half of the truth. Most of the truth.

Clay told him that by the time the baby arrived, either the baby had to be tested or the case dropped.

"What test?"

"A blood test. It was *nothing*."

"Did you have unprotected sex with her?" she asked, her face finally registering something—horror.

"No, no. I used a condom, but it broke. I swear to God, Amy, it aged me ten years—and besides, it all happened before we met." His legs, his whole body was shaking. He needed to sit down. He made his way over to a chair across the room.

She watched, immobile from the couch.

"You thought you fathered a child with who?"

What was her name? Langley had told him, but it hadn't registered.

"Some girl I met in a club."

Amy flinched. She was paper white. Was she ill?

"What?" Why was she acting like this? Busted condoms happened. If the press had gotten hold of the story, Ike was probably going nuts about now—

"What was her fucking *name*, Shane?" she said, too calmly, rising from the couch, her body stiff, hands clenched at her sides.

He got to his feet and took two steps toward her. "Whoa, babe."

She took a half step back, both fisted hands up, shaking. "Don't 'babe' me, you asshole. *What was her name?*" The words forced out from behind clenched teeth.

It was on the tip of his tongue. Carla? Krista? "I was pretty sure the baby wasn't mine."

"*Pretty sure*? And you didn't think that was important enough to bring up with me?"

He looked down.

"And you don't know her name. *Even now*. Get out. Get out of my room and out of my life." Her tone was defeated.

"Amy," he approached her carefully, speaking softly. "It was a fucked up situation."

She skirted him. "Get out."

He took another step toward her.

Expressionless no more, loathing was etched into her perfect, pale face.

He recoiled.

She went into the bedroom and dragged his bag out of the corner, threw his clothes on top of it.

He stood in the doorway, stomach churning. "Amy, please, wait."

She marched to the bathroom, he followed, only to be hit in the chest with his toiletry bag. He picked it up with nerveless fingers.

"If you don't leave now, I'll call hotel security. I don't care who finds out."

"Amy, don't do this to us." He walked into the room where she was dragging his duffel to the door.

She raised her head.

The disgust on her face laced through him.

"I didn't do anything to us. You did. You ended it with your lies and your cheating."

"I didn't—"

He froze at the foot of the bed. He saw it in her face then. It wasn't the paternity suit that had leaked. It was that girl—Erika.

"Wait, Amy, it wasn't anything."

She pulled open the door.

"I thought you were cheating on me! You weren't in your room last night; I sent people up to check."

She stared at him incredulously. "You thought I was cheating so you'd. . .what? Pay me back?"

"But I didn't—it didn't get that far. . ."

She turned her back on him, propped open the door with her arm and kicked his duffel bag out into the hall.

"Fuck off, Shane," she pointed to the hallway. "Or I'll call security."

He glanced at her face on his way out and his heart seized.

Chapter Twenty-two

Dancing with the Stars had called again. Yesterday they'd sent someone up to the tiny two-bedroom house she was renting on the outer edge of Malibu. Ike's doing, she felt sure. She'd said no, repeatedly, ever grateful to Shane's attorney for figuring out that she was owed that endorsement money and then finding it. She had enough of a nest egg to able to pay for room, board, and tuition for the next four years—longer than that. Maybe grad school, too. With the investment advisor Clay Langley had recommended, she should be able to live off the interest of the money, if she was conservative.

One month after being fired and breaking up with Shane, she was still a topic of conversation. Let them theorize that was why she left the sport, Shane, all of it. There would be no more skating, or dancing. Her orthopedist had made that clear.

Despite the surgery, she had lost mobility. She wasn't allowed to do anything high impact—maybe forever. And he'd shown her on the films the areas of her hip still affected. She could need a hip replacement, he'd warned her, and she would have arthritis—there was no question about that.

Every morning she woke up, happy for a split second, then the awareness sank in and the tears followed. She was going through life on autopilot. The only way she was able to sleep at night was to exhaust herself swimming. Physical therapy had improved her hip to where she barely limped and rarely had pain but she knew she shouldn't be driving herself to her physical limits each day.

She was ready to make good on her promise to Rowena. She's gone to see her old tutor and her family in the wake of the breakup with Shane and hadn't turned her phone on the entire week she'd stayed there. All she'd done was sleep and play with the kids. Rowena had expressed concern about her weight—her eating. How could she eat? She was heartsick.

Amy shoved her books into her bag. She didn't want to be late for her class at the community college. She wasn't enrolled—the semester was halfway over when she'd arrived in Los Angeles—so she wouldn't get credit, but she was hoping that something, some course would resonate and point her in the direction of the rest of her life. So far it hadn't happened.

She was meeting with a college counselor in a few weeks to discuss transferring credits to the state college. Maybe there was some kind of test they could give her so she could figure out the rest of her life, now that she was retired. And alone.

• • •

Shane arrived at the studio with five minutes to spare. Goddamn LA traffic. He was no longer nervous. Everything made him angry these days. The way things had ended with Amy. The fact that she wouldn't take his calls. He didn't know where she was or if she was all right—or how she was recovering.

He was pissed at Amy, pissed at this Kayla who had sent him into a tailspin when she claimed he was the father of her child, knowing full well he wasn't—she'd finally dropped the suit. And he was furious with Erika. He worked out, ran, biked, and skated— yes skated, with an underlying ferocity. He pushed himself in his workouts so hard, his trainer had asked him who he was running from, and worried that the twenty pounds he had added for the role might be in jeopardy.

He told himself he was trying to get into character before the audition, but somehow along the way he'd become Hank LaMott. An irredeemable fuckup.

The worst part was that after all the training and bulking up and skating, the role he wanted so badly, he no longer gave two shits about.

He knew what people thought of his turn as the Dark Avenger—that he'd been horribly miscast. And yet here he was, auditioning for the role of another antihero.

At least they couldn't see right through him to what he really was. Darker and sicker and shadier than anyone else.

Amy had come the closest to finding out. Even to him, his betrayal was monstrous.

She hadn't understood what she was seeing. And what she knew was only a hint at what lay beneath. She couldn't possibly love what he was, a gaping hole, one that he tried to fill with the compulsions of his body.

They called him in the room. There were nods of greeting all around. The director's face was set. He was against this whole thing—clearly Ike had applied some pressure to even get Shane in the room.

Not you.

He'd been to auditions like this before, where they had someone else in mind for the role and no matter how he played it, he had no hope. Well, fuck them.

He was here. He had memorized the lines, lived them lately. They'd picked the most harrowing scene from the script. The scene where LaMott accepted that love doesn't conquer anything and the past won't stay buried. His demons didn't just revisit him, they wreaked havoc on the lives of the people he loved, and he was powerless to halt the consequences. Unable to communicate, without the tools to move forward, his rage simmered until this scene where it boiled over.

He prepared to read the scene where he let go of the person he loved most to give her a chance at happiness—without him. Hank LaMott's only selfless act as he circled the drain allowed his lover to escape his misery. If only he'd been that selfless, he could've spared Amy the pain.

Shane was to read the part with the woman his agent told him was a shoo-in for the role of the wife. For the first time in his life, in the guise of acting, he was connected to all his shame and rage. It was hideously unpleasant and impossible to mask.

By the end of the scene the actress was as physically removed from him as she could get—damn near pressed up against the wall on the opposite side of the room as he'd stalked her. If he'd been auditioning for one of his romantic lead roles, they would've had him removed from the building.

He finished out the scene, put down the script, and walked out in a daze.

• • •

It took forever, but he tracked her down. His lawyer had all her information from the lawsuit. Shane stood in front of her run-down apartment building, shaking with rage. How had he gotten to this point in his life? If this stupid bitch hadn't filed a paternity suit, if he hadn't been so anxious and sleepless, he never would have believed Amy could cheat, he never would have gone to the bar and met up with that woman.

The dominoes wouldn't have come crashing down.

She was as good a person to vent it on as any. She must've known it was a bogus claim. He took the steps to her garden apartment two at a time, arriving at the dented and peeling door. He knocked.

No answer.

He pounded on the door, unleashing his anger.

What was that noise from the other side? It barely sounded human. Were those wails? He stepped away from the door.

And then it flung open and there she stood, bloated, eyes red-rimmed. She took two steps back with the wailing, flailing bundle in her arms. He took a step away also. They stood staring at each other.

Her shoulders slumped and she turned away, leaving the door open. He stood on the concrete walkway for a moment, then glanced behind him to ensure there were no prying eyes.

He entered the darkened apartment and flicked the light switch. Nothing.

He looked out the window. The lights were on outside someone's front door across the way.

He took another step into the room and shut the door behind him.

She sat on the stained couch, head back, and tried to get the baby onto her exposed breast. The red-faced baby screamed.

He looked away, embarrassed, but not before he'd caught site of tears leaking down her face, running into her lank hair.

Pity stirred and he quashed it.

He looked around the apartment, uncomfortable. "Power's out," he said unnecessarily.

"No shit."

God, she looked awful. Was this really the same woman he'd taken home from the club ten plus months ago?

"Why?"

"I didn't pay the bill."

And just like that, Shane was a child of ten again, afraid of the dark. There had never been enough money so Mandy juggled utility bills—one month the water would be shut off, another the power.

"What do you want?" she managed.

"An apology for fucking up my life would be a good start."

"Your life was already fucked up, but okay, I'm sorry for my part in it."

"You must've known it wasn't mine."

"There was a two-week window. It could've been anyone's. I figured my luck couldn't be that good. I hoped you'd pay me enough to go away and be quiet."

"Ah."

The face she turned to him was unutterably weary, lined with exhaustion.

"How old are you?" he asked.

"Twenty-four."

Two years younger than Amy. A stab of grief pierced him and he grimaced. When would thoughts of her cease to make him want to put holes in walls?

"You looked younger when we met."

She barked out a laugh. "Ya think? This baby shit ain't easy."

"Would you have had it, you know, if you were sure it wasn't mine?"

She was silent for four beats of his heart, then she looked up from the baby and met his gaze evenly. "I don't know. But I don't regret having her."

"Is there anyone else who might," he looked around the dismal, dark apartment—it wasn't dirty, just run down, "help out? Step up?"

"I've got a few friends who have helped out, but no family locally—thankfully. I'll manage. I always have."

She reminded him of Amy. Tough and self-reliant. But he knew what this life was like. Hell, maybe his mom had been like this before poverty had ground her down.

He blew out a sigh. "Anything I can do?"

She leaned forward, unlatching the baby, now asleep. She wrapped her gently and deposited the bundle in Shane's stiff arms. "I could use a year of sleep about now, but even half an hour would help. She won't need me for another few hours. Would you stick around? *Please.*"

He looked down in horror at the little dark-haired girl in his arms. "I don't know anything about babies," he whispered and tried to hand her back, but she refused to take the child, staring him down until he nodded, cradling the little body to him gingerly.

She stretched out on the couch and fell asleep.

He rose and walked down the dark hall into the bedroom. It all came back—the condom, the photo she'd tried to take. Panic.

He studied the room. There was a mesh playpen thing next to the bed. He carefully laid the sleeping baby in the center. The bed was made. A bureau doubled as a changing area with a pad, wipes, a few baby clothes stacked. This room was neatly arranged, too.

It would be a drop out of his bucket to help her out of this situation. Give her a leg up and see what she could make of it.

He went into the bathroom to make a few calls without waking either the girl or the baby.

• • •

He left Kayla's apartment, quietly closing the door behind him, exhausted.

The first time he'd read that script and identified with Hank LaMott, he'd assumed LaMott should've kept his distance from people. Stopped trying to reconcile with his wife and his children since he was so obviously broken. But for the first time it occurred to him that LaMott was not terribly smart—and not brave, for pushing everyone away, but never investigating his failings. He should've focused on fixing his rage, then made amends.

He'd always assumed that once he fell in love it would fill the hole in him, that his cravings for anonymous sexual encounters would stop. In the past when the compulsions hadn't gone away, he'd assumed there was some flaw in the relationship and ended it. But there was no flaw in Amy—she was the best person he'd ever known.

He loved her beyond reason. He could see that now that he'd destroyed it.

He had always been completely fucked up inside. But it didn't have to be. And maybe that was the most important thing he'd learned from her.

Her childhood and adolescence had been as difficult as or more traumatic than his. She'd had her own issues as a result, but she saved herself by doing the healthiest thing: taking the only way out and striking out on her own. Like her, he had to stop himself from going over the cliff. Whoever had written this stupid script he loved so much about isolation and desolation and pain didn't get it.

The level of intimacy he'd had with Amy was completely off the wall. Living with her. Loving her. He had a choice to make: figure out what was wrong or repeat the same mistakes ad infinitum.

Chapter Twenty-three

"Five minutes. Please," Shane asked.

Amy steeled herself and debated shutting the door in his face. For a moment she allowed herself to fantasize about slamming his assorted body parts in the door.

When would this kicked-in-the-gut feeling go away? She'd had the wind knocked out of her plenty of times in her life, she'd been assaulted, robbed, harassed, and stalked in her career. Yet none of those experiences came close to the horror of this one. She'd given this asshole her carefully guarded heart and he hadn't only stomped on it, he'd publically shredded it.

"I've made it clear that I don't want to see or hear from you. I hope to avoid looking at your face for the rest of my life."

"I'm begging you," he pleaded.

"There's nothing you could say that would change anything."

She glanced up, made it as far as the strong tanned column of his neck, watched his throat work as he swallowed.

"Please," he said again.

Amy scowled. "Let me grab a jacket." She was cold from the inside out, despite the warmth of the day. She followed him outside, giving him a wide berth as she moved past, careful not to brush up against his body. She led him down the pathway through the gate to the deck on the side of the house. There was no way she could stand to be in the same room with him. Dizziness surged through her, setting off white spots in front of her vision.

Her chest constricted.

Shoulders hunched, she perched on the edge of one of her new patio chairs.

He sat opposite her. "Cute place," he said.

She laced her fingers together tightly. Even looking at him now, there wasn't room for anger, just a stunned disbelief. Her stomach spasmed. How could her brain and her heart lead her so completely astray?

"I'm not going to sit here and make small talk with you," she managed through a throat thick with unshed tears.

"No. I know. I want you to know—"

God help her she went there. She couldn't stop the words from pouring out. "Why did you do it? Was it something I didn't have or—" Her voice broke. There it was. The thing that had been haunting her. That her love—that she herself—was somehow lacking. For all the fury directed at him, it was a raging insecurity driving it. She'd given him her heart, and he went looking elsewhere.

He made a move toward her and she shrank away.

He resettled in his chair, his expression stricken.

"God, no. No! You gave me more than I ever even hoped for, Amy. More than I deserved. You have to know it wasn't you."

She started to rise.

He put a hand up. "I didn't think I'd get caught. Or maybe I was hoping I'd get caught. Despite everything, I wasn't able to rein in this ... the part of me that gets its fucked up kicks with strangers. There's something wrong with *me*. I tried so hard with you. I didn't want to do it. I managed to talk myself out of so much of my bad behavior while I was with you. But in the end, I ... I couldn't resist the temptation."

Bile rose and she clenched her teeth. She finally dared to look at his face. This time he was the one who couldn't meet her eyes. He looked drawn, older than his twenty-nine years.

"I don't know what I'm supposed to say to that." She stood.

"I fucked up and I'm sorry. I have some understanding of why I did it. Not that it will make any sense to you. It was never about you."

Furious and dry-eyed she stared down at his blonde hair glinting in the sun. This golden wreck of a man who had permanently damaged her heart. "The fuck it isn't."

He looked up briefly, his eyes red-rimmed, his face a pasty white beneath his tan.

"There's always temptation when you're in a relationship. It's not like you don't notice other people. You make a decision to be faithful and don't put yourself in harm's way," she said.

"I'm trying to tell you that somewhere along the way, sex went from because I can to because I can't stop," he managed hoarsely, still unable to meet her gaze.

She stood frozen with disbelief. "What?"

"I don't drink much or use drugs or … or any of that. Instead I have sex. Compulsively. With a lot of different people. I always have. There have been so many women since I was a teenager. And it's meaningless. And it doesn't feel good. Not during and definitely not after. It's been this way for most of my adult life. Until you."

"What are you trying to say? That you're some kind of addict? Please," she scoffed. "Why is it if a guy can't keep his dick in his pants, it has to be labeled an addiction?"

"All I can tell you is my experience with sex, Amy. And I'm done trying to excuse it. It doesn't matter why I use sex with strangers, only that I stop."

She sneered. "This is bullshit."

He ignored her comment, continuing, haltingly. "My sexual compulsions have jeopardized my career, wreaked havoc on relationships at every level. You recognized that early on, you saw right through me. In Tennessee you called me on it in that hotel room. But you got it wrong, Amy—it's not that I hate women. I hate myself. And," he inhaled, "it got worse while I was with you. I was happier with you, had more of a connection with you than anyone else ever in my life, and it was still *there*. I haven't had sex with anyone else since I've been with you. But … "

Here it comes. Those white spots danced in front of her eyes again and her body suffused with heat.

Oh shit, I should've eaten.

She went to her knees on the deck.

Shane rushed over. "Amy? What's wrong?" He put a hand on her back.

She shrank away. Her vision still hadn't cleared so she stretched her legs out in front of her and laid down until her head rested on her knees, heart racing. She turned her clammy face toward Shane and he gasped.

"Jesus, Amy, are you sick? You're so pale and ... thin."

She closed her eyes. "I'm lightheaded."

He kneeled next to her. "Should I get you some juice or something? I have a soda in the car ... "

"I don't have much in the house." *You don't have anything in the house.*

He disappeared for a few minutes and came back with a warm Coke.

She sat up and took the drink from him as he knelt next to her on the patio.

He rubbed his face with his hands, a face contorted by anguish. "I shouldn't have come here like this, dumping all this on you ... "

"How many times, Shane? How many women were there?"

This time his red-rimmed eyes did meet hers. "I haven't had sex with anyone but you since we started dating. But I have done things ... things I'm ashamed of."

Amy pressed her lips together, tears stinging her eyes. "Like?"

"Sexting, touching ... no kissing, no undressing."

"Sex?"

"No. I swear it, Amy. But the things I did were things I shouldn't have done in a committed relationship with you. And my therapist says—"

She raised disbelieving eyes to his face, "You have a therapist?"

"Yeah. Since a few weeks ago. And he tells me I need to be honest with you about where I am, and where I'm going if … this is going to work," he said, haltingly.

She pulled her legs to her chest and wrapped her arms around them.

"This?" She gestured between them. "*This* is over."

He hung his head, defeated.

"But I deserve to know everything. Who, what, when. . ."

He looked at her. "I don't know who. That's part of my … thing. I don't know them, other than a first name sometimes and almost never the same person twice. It's not as," he paused, "thrilling. But that woman they got pictures of at the bar … it wasn't the first time I'd been out there, trolling. And I'd been close a few times. Really close. But I always pulled back before I took that final step. Before I went home with someone."

She shook her head. "Is it because I was unavailable when I was on the road?"

"No. Normal people can stay celibate for weeks or months or years in a committed relationship, Amy. It's not about you," he repeated.

She knew he had issues, major issues, but she'd let herself believe he cared about her. That she was different, that they had something. And now he was pinning his infidelity on *this*? He said he was taking responsibility, but blaming it on some compulsion or addiction wasn't taking responsibility. Nor was it telling her what she needed to know. *What is it about me that couldn't satisfy you?*

He spread his hands. "Amy, the relationship I had with you was unlike any I've had with a woman. I hadn't experienced intimacy like that. Even the *way* we did it—missionary, you remember how much that freaked me out the first time? I never wanted that, and now that's my favorite way to be close to you. To wrap you up in my body, while I'm so deep inside you, you pull every bad thing out." He gave a bitter laugh. "Sex with you wasn't shameful and didn't leave me feeling empty afterward. I never made that connection before, maybe because I've never been capable of true intimacy. But in spite of that, I couldn't control all the other shit … the temptation, the obsession. I wanted to—God! I quit the porn, stopped going to the sites—"

"Porn?" What man with the kind of life he had used porn? Porn was for guys who couldn't get laid, not guys like Shane who could win a national championship in a sexathalon.

"Yeah. I've spent a lot of time online doing that. I stopped looking at it after we got serious. I told myself it was because I didn't want you to have something pop up when you used my computer or catch me, but I stopped because I didn't want to use it anymore. "

She was sure the shock and horror must be reflected on her face. Revulsion had replaced anger.

"My attitudes toward sex are incredibly screwed up. It started back when TruAchord was touring. They'd have parties. . ."

Her stomach churned and she tried another sip of the Coke, her gaze never leaving his face.

He rubbed a hand across his face. "Fans. Uh, women, though, not girls."

This had to be the sickest thing she'd ever heard. "Groupies?"

He shrugged.

"Oh my God. And your parents had nothing to say to this?"

"My parents weren't around. And the label didn't want the legal problems of us dating underage girls when we were with TruAchord—'cause you know, with our fan base … so they would facilitate … things."

She was sure the revulsion inside was reflected on her face. "Who did?"

He pressed his lips together. "Well, the tour manager, people like that. And it was like parties, but yeah, we were all getting laid.

I didn't have a regular girlfriend until I was twenty. And you know what it's like on the road, casual or nothing."

She nodded.

"In my twenties, when I stopped traveling, I met people in clubs and stuff. But old habits die hard and when I got into something, I wasn't faithful. Not to anyone for any length of time. I didn't ask for it and I didn't offer it, until you."

"That's pathetic."

He nodded. "I thought I'd be able to give it up—all of it— when I met the right person. That love would fix what was wrong with me." He looked up at her, his face drawn. "But it didn't. And that's not love's fault, because I love you so fucking much, Amy."

She blanched. "You don't love me like I loved you," she whispered.

He took her hand, his grip painful.

She withdrew it with a wince.

His expression was tortured. "I loved you then, and I love you now. More than anything. You're the one who kept telling me how all the problems in my life—the naked picture, the paternity suit, the career problems, right down to my relationship with my sister and her husband—was all because I don't have a healthy relationship with sex." He took her hands again. "You were the one who pointed it out time after time, so why is it so hard for you to believe that it isn't you or how much I love you?"

Her lips twisted. She'd thought all his problems revolved around women—but it was deeper than that. The dots had all been there; she hadn't connected them.

"I know you must be so disgusted with me. Trust me, it pales in comparison to how ashamed I am. What I've become is ... revolting. I knew when I was hanging over the abyss by my fingernails night after night while you were on the road that I'd hurt you. But if you believe nothing else I'm telling you, please believe that it wasn't anything lacking in you. You're amazing."

His voice broke and when he spoke again, it was hoarse. "You were dealt the same crappy hand I was, family-wise, and yet you've adapted and thrived. I've wallowed. If that picture hadn't busted me … but I'm getting better."

She was already shaking her head. She couldn't get sucked back into this. "The trust is gone, Shane."

But underneath the anger and humiliation and disgust was a tiny kernel of pity. There was something about the way he described hanging onto the edge of the cliff by his fingernails. The idea of him with other women, touching them while he professed to care for her—it made her want to hurl.

And stab him with something.

"I've tried over the years to be in relationships, and with me there are two options: open or over. I end stuff because I don't want to cheat. And I've had some success with open relationships, but they usually go bad too. That wasn't even something I considered with you, because the idea of you with another man sickens me."

"Yeah? Then you know how it feels."

He nodded. "I was in agony over Kyle for a long time."

She groaned. "For the love of God, Shane, we may as well be siblings."

"I know, I know. My head knows that, but I have a jealous streak a mile wide where you are concerned. The therapist has been quick to point out the irony."

"I'm sorry, but I can't be with someone who can't be faithful."

He looked gutted. There was no other word for it. He held up a shaking hand. "I think if I do the work, I can be … if you could—"

"I'd like you to leave, please."

"I'm fixing it."

"I'm sure you are, but I can't take that chance."

"Why not?" She watched his throat work as he swallowed. "Because you don't love me?" He released her hands.

She wrapped her arms around herself. That wasn't it. Despite everything she still loved him. Didn't understand him, wanted to kill him, but she loved him.

"My therapist thought you, of all people, might understand."

She recoiled. "Me? God, Shane, what did you tell him? I've slept with a handful of people but ... but not like *that*."

"Not sex, your eating disorder."

His face crumpled as his gaze swept her body.

She stared, uncomprehending.

Oh.

That's why what he was saying sounded so familiar. The hanging on by the fingernails. This was no heartache diet, this was her anorexia and exercise bulimia rearing its ugly head again after all these years. She hadn't taken her recovery seriously, not for a long time. She'd managed with a meeting or some calls here and there during the last few years. But the emotional toll of the end of her career, the cheating, her injury. How could she have missed this?

She looked down at her body, seeing it, really seeing it for the first time. And it all fit together. The crazy self-talk she'd engaged in with her "I'm too heartbroken to eat" and "I'm not skating so I may as well kill myself with three-hour swims and extra physical therapy" excuses.

Here she was, standing at the bottom of the mountain again, like she'd been at seventeen.

My God. I'm right back to where I was before I left the circuit. Only this time instead of "if I were thinner, I could win it all," it's "my hip wouldn't have gone bad." Or, "if I were thinner, he wouldn't have cheated."

She barely recognized herself. How had she dropped so much weight so fast? And it was all a delusion. There was no control—not over food or exercise, not over him or her life—and the decisions about her future that had to be made.

Who did she think she was to judge him? Or Becky for that matter. She was deeply mired in the mud of her addiction and denial.

Tears filled her eyes as she stared at him.

He knew, he must've seen it immediately.

"I'm as fucked up as you are," she said brokenly.

Worry mixed with hope ignited in his indigo eyes and they bored into her. "I thought you might understand. No matter how much I love you, you aren't going to fix what's wrong with me, the way I can't fix you. I have to do that work myself. The way you do. In therapy. With support."

He offered her another sip of the Coke and she took it.

"There are support groups for sex addiction?"

"My therapist suggested I avoid the groups and work one on one with him. He's well-known in the field, but there is inpatient rehab—"

"For *sex*?"

His lips quirked briefly. "You don't read the entertainment magazines, do you? I've known people in the industry who have been in rehab for sex addiction, gambling, you name it. The guy I'm seeing thinks we don't need to go there, that sessions should get me where I need to be, if I'm willing to work at it. And I am. Please, Amy. Give me another chance. I can't make too many promises here, but I love you and I'll be honest with you."

Looking into that beautiful, ravaged face, she desperately wanted to trust him, believe him.

He took her hand again, gently, staring down at her fingers.

A shiver rode through her body, as she sat, paralyzed with indecision.

He took a shuddering breath and looked up.

"No promises?" she asked.

"Other than my love for you and being honest with you about my feelings, the therapist advises against it."

Yeah. That's pretty much how her program had worked. One day at a time.

"I need time to process all this and … to get myself back on track."

He sat back on his heels and took her hand. "I know. Take whatever time you need. I'll be here, when you're ready—if you're ready."

He came back an hour later with three sacks of groceries. She watched him from the window as he set them on the stoop. Then he returned to his car and drove off. Tears filled her eyes as she got out of the chair, the dizziness and fatigue making sense, and brought the food in.

Chapter Twenty-four

She walked into a quaint stucco cottage with the tiny sign on the front door listing the four counselors. She'd chosen someone at random, but when she'd called, the woman told her they had two specialists in eating disorders and compulsive and addictive behaviors. She settled herself on to the floral couch in a cheerful waiting room and played with her phone. She hadn't been to therapy in ages. More than five years. Occasional meetings, journaling, and calls had been enough to keep her disorder at bay. Or so she'd thought.

"Amy?" A tall woman in chinos and a Ramones t-shirt with a very short, chic gray hair came to the entryway of the hall. "Hi, I'm Elizabeth."

Amy shook her hand.

"Follow me."

The woman ushered her into a room that was probably a bedroom at one time but now sported two well-worn comfy chairs and a loveseat separated by a coffee table with a box of tissue, a few coasters, and reading glasses. There was a small fridge and a coffee pot in one corner.

"Can I get you anything?" Elizabeth asked, walking over to the fridge and opening the door. "I have coffee—just made. Water, soda?"

"I'm good, thanks."

The woman grabbed a manila file from her desk. "I have your info here." She put on her glasses and thumbed through the file. Frowning, she looked up at Amy.

"I should tell you I know your name. Figure skating is a sport I follow."

She shrugged.

"And I'm very familiar with some of the issues that plague athletes in your sport as well as dance, gymnastics." She waved a hand. "So I want you to feel comfortable talking with me, Amy. You mentioned on the phone wanting a therapist who had treated people with eating disorders. I'm well-versed in that area and treat a number of patients with those same issues." She leaned forward and looked her directly in the eye. "I'd like to help in any way I can."

She nodded, readjusting her position on the couch.

By the time Amy walked out of her one-hour appointment that had turned into two, she was reeling. Apparently the woman was well-versed in everything. She'd helped couples and families deal with addictions of every type. So Shane's claim was the real deal and not unique for all that. Elizabeth had classified him as a garden variety sex addict based on what Amy had relayed. The woman wasn't shocked or horrified by anything Amy told her.

Most importantly, this woman knew eating disorders, understood the control issues, and hadn't let her leave without assurances of daily meetings and sponsorship.

• • •

Amy examined the attractive young woman standing on her porch through the screen. She met the woman's eyes, then looked down at the little baby asleep in the carrier. That infant looked nothing like Shane with its slightly olive skin tone and dark, almost black hair. The baby didn't look anything like the girl standing in front of her either. The paternity test was a technicality, but he probably hadn't known that. Had the girl?

"I'm not with him," Amy said.

"I know," the young woman said softly, shifting her feet.

She couldn't leave them out on her porch. She pushed open the screen door. "C'mon in."

The woman picked up the carrier, careful not to disturb the sleeping baby, and brought her into the living room. "Pets?"

Amy shook her head.

"Can we go out on the porch and talk?"

Amy looked in askance at the child.

"She ate an hour ago. We both did. She'll sleep for a while yet."

The hostess in her would not be suppressed—even for Shane's ex-lover. "Get you anything? Water? Coffee?" she asked.

"I'd love a coffee, but I'll drink water." The woman pulled a canister out of her bag. Amy led the way to the porch and curled up into the wicker chair, pulling her legs up under her chin.

The other woman sat. "I'm Kayla."

"Amy."

They studied each other in silence.

"I hear you're a great skater."

She shook her head and attempted a smile through stiff lips. "Gross exaggeration."

The silence lengthened and grew painful.

Amy studied her knees, avoiding looking at the woman opposite her. Kayla was beautiful. Her body, fantastic. Skinny with huge breasts—but maybe that was from nursing? She pushed those thoughts away. It was one thing to know about Shane's past. It was another thing to have it sitting in all its glory on her front porch. And was it his past?

"So, I'm sure you're wondering why I'm here."

She met her stare evenly. "Yep."

"Shane's been ... helping me out."

Her stomach lurched and nausea overwhelmed her. She took a few calming breaths. When she spoke her voice shook. "I thought the baby wasn't his."

Kayla frowned. "It isn't. He's helping me because ... well, I don't know why he's helping me."

Amy looked her up and down, eyebrows raised.

The other woman chortled. "That? Please. As if I'd want a guy near me now. No, you misunderstand. He came to see me two months ago to scream at me for ruining his life."

"Oh?" Amy rubbed damp palms on her jeans.

"Yeah. He showed up at my place after I had to drop the lawsuit. He was furious. And I was so exhausted, I didn't give a shit, you know? And I felt bad about what I did to him so I let him get it off his chest," she said candidly. "I knew it probably wasn't his baby early on. I wanted it to be—I needed the money and I figured he might pay me to keep quiet. There was that busted condom. And I read the papers; I knew you guys broke up."

"You weren't the reason we broke up."

"No?" She looked puzzled, then the light dawned. "Oh. Yeah. The pictures with that girl?" She shrugged. "Some guys, that's how they deal with their shit—the stress or whatever. I'm not giving him a pass or anything, but I think what I did—the lawsuit, refusing to get the blood test—it ate at him and he freaked out. God, you should have seen him when he came to visit me—sweating and shaking and enraged." She shrugged. "What a mess. Look, I'm not doing this very well, I haven't slept more than three hours in an age and it's hard to string two words together."

"If it's not his baby, why is he helping you?"

The woman frowned at whatever she saw on Amy's face. "Not because he wants me or something. Believe me, he doesn't. And he doesn't owe me anything since Jazmin's not his. For some reason, he decided to help me out. Pity? Kindness? I don't know. He found me a guest house on his friend's property. The friend is never there—I think he's in Vegas? Anyway, Shane's friend made me the property manager or some bullshit like that. But basically I live there for free. It's not forever. The guy will probably sell, but the market for mansions tanked apparently, so he had it on, now he's taken it off. In the meantime it's more than I could have ever dreamed of. A safe neighborhood and part-time job where I can take care of my kid and feed us. Shane put a nursery in the second bedroom—got all the stuff. All of it. I had nothing. I mean, can you see him at Babies R Us?"

She leaned forward, her eyes locked on Kayla.

"So I fucked up his life and this is what he does for me. Helping some girl he doesn't know who tried to screw him over—a couple of times actually. I tried to get a naked picture of him that night."

She sat back in her chair with a snort.

Kayla grinned. "Yeah. Anyway. I'm not that stupid girl anymore. And he's not that asshole who only thought about his dick. You know? And I ... I was hoping you'd give him another chance. 'Cause girl, he has been *wrecked* over your breakup."

"Kayla—"

A muffled cry came through the window and she froze, listening intently. "It's too soon," she muttered. The house remained silent and Kayla's shoulders relaxed.

"The guy is crazy about you. Give him another chance? I feel guilty about my part in all of this."

"Did he put you up to this?"

"Fuck no. He would never. But I thought I might try to help him after he's helped me so much."

Amy nodded.

"I can imagine that—well, it's hard to forgive. But the way he talks about you and how freakin' sad he is. . ."

"It's not so simple, Kayla. The cheating, his history—it's not great."

Kayla nodded sagely. "Oh, I hear ya, girlfriend. It's not like I've never been with cheaters. Or given them a second chance, y'know? I've been burned plenty. But some people are worth it. And that's what I came here to tell you. He's worth it."

"Well." Amy stood. "Thanks for coming."

Chapter Twenty-five

Amy settled into the gunmetal gray folding seat with barely a twinge. She hadn't been in a skating rink since she left Enchanted. And she hadn't seen Shane since he'd come to see her eight weeks ago. She'd Googled him once—no new scandals.

She'd called Ike to tell him in no uncertain terms that she was putting her health first for once. *Dancing with the Stars* was out, and so were all the reality TV shows he'd tried to push on her. He'd huffed and puffed and complained that she didn't need an agent.

She'd asked after Shane, and Ike told her he'd passed on the hockey role offer.

"Why?"

"Damned if I know. After all I did to get him that audition, they offered him the part and he turned it down. Said he didn't want to wallow for a year. Took some sci-fi military comedy instead."

"Oh my God, not the role of the army captain?"

"Yeah, you heard about it?"

"No, I mean, I read the script. I thought Shane would be perfect."

"Well, someone agreed with you—or wanted the marquee name or whatever. He starts shooting in a few months. If he can pull himself away from that amateur hockey league he's in."

"He's still doing that?"

"Yes. God knows why, I've told him to quit—anything but that. The idea of a puck to that face gives me nightmares."

Amy hung up the phone, dazed.

Shane was still playing on the Los Angeles Stars quadruple E hockey league. It hadn't taken much sleuthing to find their practice schedule.

And there he was, warming the bench. He was easy to identify—tall and broad-shouldered, his blonde hair still on the long side, glinting under his helmet, waiting for his turn. Her heart leaped when he stood, hopped over the rail, and glided onto the ice.

She was making strides in her recovery, had regained some weight. She had a sponsor and a tight knit community in her recovery program. She'd been accepted into three of the four-year colleges she'd applied to locally, and now that she had a course plotted that would lead to a degree in counseling, she couldn't wait to start in the fall.

Kyle and the rest of her friends would be arriving in town this week, wrapping up their Enchanted season.

Even from her vantage point she could see Shane's focus. His skating was so much improved, she couldn't believe it. Despite his efforts, it was apparent that coordinating the stick and the puck out on the ice was still a real challenge. He took the complaints and ribbing of his teammates in stride after the other team scored against him.

What he lacked in skill he made up for in intensity. There were only half a dozen people in the place watching, and Amy had taken care to sit halfway up the bleachers, so she wouldn't be easily spotted.

She loved him. Despite her best efforts to scour him from her heart, there he remained.

The referee blew the whistle for a break and Shane joined his team, laughing and joking as they rehydrated and leaned against the rails. One of the men in the group made eye contact with Amy and grinned. The thickset man shouldered Shane and toasted her with his raised sports drink.

Shane looked up and their eyes met. The grin disappeared, and his face hardened.

Her welcoming smile faded. She watched as he took the stadium stairs in his skates.

She made her way to the aisle to meet him.

The words of greeting died in her throat as he approached. Jaw set, the hard angles and plane of his face flushed with the heat and sweat of exertion. Was he angry? His two hands came down on her shoulders like manacles as he dragged her to him. She raised her head and his mouth came down on hers. The kiss tasted of salt, desperation, and hope mingled together in a searing explosion of intensity. His tongue pushed into her mouth and Amy moaned. Shane took one step down, too tall in his skates. His mouth left hers and he kissed her cheeks, her chin, her forehead, then rested his sweaty brow against hers.

He leaned back, his blue gaze boring into hers. "God, I love you, Amy Astor."

"I love you, too."

He gaze swept down her body critically. "Better," he said, relief evident in his tone. She felt the heat rise in her neck.

"Am I not supposed to say anything? Not supposed to notice?" he asked. "I don't know the etiquette."

"I'm improving," she admitted.

"Good. It scared the crap out of me, seeing you like that."

"And you?" Despite that kiss, she had to know.

He never broke eye contact. "I'm single and abstinent. There's been no one, nothing with anyone since you."

"Is that how it works?" she asked. "I don't know the etiquette for you, either."

"I'm only supposed to have sex as part of a healthy relationship—but since I don't want to have a relationship with anyone but you, I haven't had sex," he said bluntly.

Amy fought a grin. "Then I guess you are doubly glad to see me."

"I want to love you and only you for the rest of my life," he said, "starting now."

"Maybe that should wait until after practice," she said, smiling as the referee blew the whistle to signal the restart of the scrimmage.

More from This Author
(From *Rock Him* by Rachel Cross)

Asher Lowe lay atop his buttery-soft, Egyptian cotton sheets, sandwiched between two women. The brunette on his right snored delicately into the pillow, exposing a booty so spectacular it was said to be insured by Lloyd's of London. Last year's Miss November, a stacked, all-natural blonde, was curled up to his left, hogging the covers.

Clubbing most of the night and living out every man's fantasy into the wee hours was easier ten years ago. Well, the recovery from the all-nighters was certainly easier back then. The part in bed was easier then. Getting women into bed? Thanks to money, a wall full of platinum albums, and a couple of Grammys, that part was easier now.

Asher lifted his head and immediately regretted it. His head throbbed from all the damn Hennessy. Would he *ever* learn not to drink with rappers?

He glanced at the clock on the nightstand and did a double take. Eight A.M.? Why on earth was he up so early?

Bzzz.

Asher cringed. The headache reached nightmarish proportions and nausea rushed up as he broke out in a cold sweat.

More buzzing. What was that? Had some device been left on?

He sat up gingerly, moving to his knees, swallowing back bile, careful not to disturb either of the bed's occupants. The brunette stirred and he froze. He didn't have it in him for round three. Hell, he wasn't sure he had it in him to make it to the bathroom.

Asher's gaze swept the floor. Strewn about the plush, cream carpet was an assortment of satin underthings, an empty box of condoms, a pair of black thigh-high boots and a lacy, red thong. La Perla, by the looks of it. No vibrating paraphernalia.

He frowned. More buzzing. Coming from the corner of the room.

He inched his way to the bottom of the bed and stood. A wave of dizziness swept through him and he rested his hands on naked thighs, biting back a moan. Things were way worse vertical. Getting back to sleep would be impossible until he turned off whatever it was.

He spied his phone on the dresser, the telltale light coming on as the insistent noise started again. His brows went up. His phone? Who the hell would be calling at the crack of dawn? Must be a wrong number.

Only a handful of people even had his private cell number, and not one of them would call before noon.

The brunette mumbled something. Snagging his phone, he hustled to the bathroom. He put the phone down and rifled through the cabinets in search of some kind of hangover remedy. He tried a sip of water with a pink-stuff chaser. God. He had been here countless times over the years and it was never worth it.

Examining his reflection in the mirror, he saw the lines that marked years of exposure to the California sun and the inexorable march to forty. Bags and circles highlighted bloodshot eyes. Leaning against the vanity countertop, he cast a glance over his shoulder at the bathroom. Why were there towels all over the floor and a bottle of bubbles overturned, leaking clear goo — ?

Oh yeah. The two in his bed had wanted to play in his hot-tub sized bathtub.

His phone vibrated on the counter and he picked it up to stare blearily at the display. Six missed calls and six voice-mail messages from a familiar Vegas number.

Asher's mouth twisted. His father knew his cell number? Interesting. Finishing in the bathroom, he stumbled out to the bedroom where he hauled on last night's jeans. Shutting the door carefully behind him, he padded to the kitchen.

Dealing with Sterling Lowe would require coffee — in vast quantities.

He set the phone on the counter and pulled out the beans. The phone vibrated again. With a glare that renewed the throbbing in his head, he picked it up.

"Yeah?" he drawled.

"Asher." His father's voice was raspy.

Asher tensed.

Sterling Lowe drew a ragged breath. "Asher … I … I don't know how to tell you this. I … I hate to do it on the phone … "

His hand clenched into a fist, a cold, hard knot formed in his stomach. "Are you sick?"

"It's Delilah."

Delilah — Dee — Asher's half-sister.

His body grew cold. The hair on the back of his neck stood up.

"What?" he whispered.

His father choked back tears, voice rough. "She was killed by a drunk driver in a head-on."

Asher collapsed onto a barstool.

"Ella?" he asked.

"She's here. I have her this weekend. Dee … Dee had a girls' weekend … I … haven't told Ella. I don't know what to do."

Some part of Asher could not believe his father had said that. Sterling Lowe always knew exactly what to do, or at least thought he did.

His father took a deep breath. "Can you come?"

"Of course." He gritted his teeth. He loved Dee. God knows he had been a better brother to her than Sterling had been a father. It was on the tip of his tongue to say something caustic when he heard a muffled sound. Asher pulled the phone from his ear and stared at it. Through all the divorces, the battles, in thirty-seven years, he had never heard his father weep. He put the phone back to his ear. "I'll be there as soon as I can."

"The jet is fueled up and ready at LAX. I sent a car — "

"I'm on my way."

"Wait. Asher?"

"Yes?"

"What do I tell," his voice was thick with tears, "Ella?"

"Can you wait until I get there?" He knew exactly who to call.

The older man let out a long, relieved sigh. "Okay. Dee wasn't supposed to pick her up until later today."

"I'll see you soon."

Ella. With no father in the picture, what would happen to her?

His lips tightened and his hands formed fists. He'd be damned if he let his father ruin another childhood.

Asher hung up the phone and dialed Justin. He had been Asher's assistant for ten years. Next to Dee, Justin Montoya was the closest thing to family he had.

"*Asher*? What the hell? It's eight — "

"I know." He managed to speak through a throat half closed by unshed tears. "It's Dee." He gritted his teeth against a wave of grief, afraid if he said the words they would become true. "She was killed in a car accident in Vegas this morning."

"What? *Oh God*, Asher, not Dee — "

"I need to go," he interrupted before the sympathy in his friend's voice made him lose the slim bit of control he had left. "The plane is waiting. Do I have a bag packed somewhere?"

"Hall closet. What about Ella?"

"She's okay. She's with my dad." A thump from upstairs made him squeeze his eyes shut in frustration. "Listen, there's a couple of girls here. Can you — "

"I got it covered man, you just go."

"Thanks," he said.

Ten minutes later, the car arrived and Asher's hands had finally stopped shaking. Memories of his younger sister flashed before him. Ruthlessly, he pushed them away. He sent a group text to a handful of friends.

Dee killed in car accident. Headed to Vegas.

Better they hear it from him than from the news.

He put his bag in the trunk of the long, sleek, black limousine, nodded his thanks to the driver holding the door open and climbed into the rear seat.

Ella.

Delilah had become pregnant with Ella in her mid-twenties when she was still thoroughly enmeshed in partying with other children of the ultra-rich. It was a scene Asher avoided. A scene he tried unsuccessfully to extricate his sister from.

Knowing Dee's crowd during that time, he was pretty sure the men she hung out with would either be horrified by the idea of becoming a daddy or thrilled for all the wrong reasons. Knocking up the daughter of one of the richest men in America had its advantages.

Asher had asked once, gently, about the father and Delilah told him she didn't know. He left it alone. Having a baby changed Dee. She had renewed purpose and vitality; being a mom and a good mom was everything to her.

He made the call to Kate Sawyer, wife of his best friend, Alec. Kate was a nurse and ran a foundation for terminally ill parents with dependent children. She and her sister had lost their mother at a young age. If anyone could answer questions about how to deal with Ella and grief, it was Kate.

He filled Kate in on the events of the morning, forcing the words out through numb lips.

"Oh, no, Asher." Her breath hitched.

"I've got to get on a plane in a few minutes and when I get there I need to know what to tell Ella."

"Oh Asher," her voice shook, "I'm so sorry. I can't imagine what you're going through."

Asher heard Alec in the background, asking questions.

Kate shushed him. "What is Ella now? Five? Six?"

"Five."

Kate sighed. "The first thing you need to know is that her understanding of death will be limited."

"What does that mean?"

"Understanding death is a process at that age. She'll only understand what her mother's death means as she gets older."

"I'm not following you, Kate." Asher's control was slipping and he knew he sounded impatient.

"You need to explain to her in very simple terms that her mother died. She'll need to be told that death is nothing like sleep, and that her mom is not coming back. She'll cry and grieve but … it'll take time. Even once you think she understands, she will probably ask for her. Sometimes it takes months or longer for a child that age to grasp that Mom isn't coming back."

Oh God. She was going to be asking when Delilah would be *back?* He fought another upwelling of grief mixed with acute nausea. "Children can also think something they've done or haven't done may have caused the death … "

"*What?*" he ground out through a stiff jaw, "that's insane."

"Asher, they don't think like we do. They aren't mini-adults. She'll need constant, patient reassurance. There are therapists who can help with this. I know a few excellent ones in LA. I'll call this morning if you like."

"God. Yes. Thanks, Kate."

There was a long pause.

"Asher?"

"Yeah?"

Kate waded in. "We're here for you. Anything you need. Anything. Help. Visits. We loved Dee. You know we love you and Ella. And we understand your feelings toward your father."

Only a handful of people knew about his conflict-ridden relationship with his father; Sterling and Asher put on a good front in public.

He loved Ella because she was his sister's kid, but he had no interest in kids of his own. None at all. Not now at any rate. But Ella? My God. And his dad? No fucking way. He would not have her grow up the way he and Dee had, in a fractured family with a distant, disinterested parent. He would get the best people. He could set her up with a full-time nanny, the best schools. *He* could figure it out, not his dad.

Asher swallowed convulsively. "I know, Kate."

"We'll see you in a few hours, we'll be flying in from Cielito."

"See you in Vegas." Asher disconnected the phone and buried his face in his hands, finally giving in to grief.

In the mood for more Crimson Romance?
Check out *Secretly* by Debra Kayn at *CrimsonRomance.com*.